SHAMELESS
St. Martin Family Saga

Gina

Watson

ISBN-13: 978-1941059050

CONTENTS

ACKNOWLEDGMENTS

Several people made this endeavor possible. Without their support this fictional world would not exist. Thank you for all the motivation and support. Beth Hill at *A Novel Edit* is wonderfully professional and does a marvelous job with the editing process. Emily Colter and Maxamaris Hoppe at Waxcreative truly did an awesome job at conceptual design for the website that channels the St. Martin Family. Damonza.com handled cover design and formatting. Mom and Karen, thank you for always agreeing to proofread. Monica your continued support and motivation were priceless on this project. Beth B. thank you for always giving it to me straight, this is invaluable to an author. To all my students and friends, this would not have happened without your beta skills: Kayla H., Courtney W., Danielle S., Meagan W., Ruth L., Angelica L., Jenna L., Tammy S., Kelli R., Amber S. Brian, what can I say, you put up with me, for that there are no words. Thank you.

CHAPTER 1

Corrigan St. Martin was balls deep in his client's owner as he had her bent over the examination table and plowed into her from behind. Cory was about to come and judging by the moans coming from Mrs. Simms, she had to be just about there too. She was married, and he shouldn't have responded to her eye-fucking him, but damn, when she'd bent over to place her cat on the table, he'd lost it. She wore a silk lace undershirt, and her breasts nearly spilled out onto the examination table with the cat. She was natural, and Cory loved that. His dick had gone hard instantly. He wondered what kind of idiot she was married to. The guy obviously wasn't aware of what he had.

Cory reached around and filled his hands with her soft shapely tits and pounded away, emptying his seed into the condom he wore. He hated the damn things but at the rate he was having sex, he couldn't afford to not wear them.

Since he'd been back in Whisky Cove, he'd been set up with an endless supply of women. They had brought in their pets for "checkups." Hell, even at church the Southern mamas threw their daughters at him. It was no secret that the St. Martin men were a catch, if one could be snagged. The only one hitched now was Cal, the youngest at twenty-six. Cory had a year on him.

There was no way Cory would let himself be roped by a nagging wife; he had too much of a good thing going. Plus he didn't need that aggravation. He recalled Camp's issues with his first wife and those with his current girlfriend, soon to be fiancée. He thought Camp was crazy. Determined to be married and settled, he'd committed to a woman the church elders had deemed "quite the catch" just because she came from an old-money family and had a strong standing in the community. But that couldn't be enough, at least not for Cory. Standing and money, no matter how high or how

1

deep, meant nothing if the woman was a ballbuster. Cory had no interest in marriage. Trying to keep a woman happy proved damn near impossible. Even his father hadn't been able to do it. Cory grunted; now he was thinking of his mom. Not the time for that. He thrust deep, trying to clear his mind. Just thinking of his mother roiled his stomach.

He recalled the day she'd left and the gut-wrenching pain she'd caused as he'd begged her not to leave. He'd been twelve and she'd been immune to his cries. Too bad he hadn't been immune to her defection.

And there he was, thinking of her again. He tweaked Mrs. Simms nipples, trying to keep his mind on business. When she moaned, he knew he'd done something right.

He'd been called the most handsome of the St. Martin men, but he didn't buy it. They all had the trademark St. Martin ice blue eyes fringed in dark lashes, something the ladies loved. They also seemed to love his hair. He was tempted to chop it off but when woman after woman locked fingers in it when he rode them, he didn't want to mess with a sure thing. The looks, coupled with his height and muscle, meant he never had to work too hard to have a woman visit his bed.

He'd lost count of the number of different women he'd given it to since his return from college last year. He was having sex daily, some days multiple times, and with a different woman every time. Nice-looking women too. He asked no questions, but he knew some of them were married, like Mrs. Simms, who was currently in the throes of orgasm.

Once Cory finished, he withdrew from Mrs. Simms, removed the condom, and threw it in the waste bin. He washed his hands while she adjusted her clothing. Opening the examination room door, Cory cleared his throat. "Mrs. Simms, bring the little guy back in four weeks for the next round of vaccinations."

Cory walked from the room and was straightening his tie when he met the tortured green eyes of a young woman holding an Airedale terrier in her arms. She sniffled as large fat tears splashed from her eyes and onto the dog.

Cory motioned her to the back examination room. Since it was time to close, his secretary, and one of his first conquests since coming home, was closing up for the day.

"Cory, she hasn't checked in."

Why was she still here? He'd told her to leave when he'd discovered the school bus had dropped off her two heathen children. She never disciplined them and she allowed them to run amuck in his clinic, treating the maze of exam rooms as a playground. Her mother must have come for them because if they were here, he'd certainly hear them.

"That's okay, Amanda, I'll take care of it. Lock up when you leave."

Truth be told, Amanda's fake tan, fake tits, and fake platinum hair gave

Cory the chills now, and her shrill voice made his skin crawl.

She sighed louder than necessary. "Okay, Cory, you have a good one."

To claim Cory as hers, Amanda had tried all the tricks women try when attempting to get their hooks into a man. One morning Cory was answering email at his desk and the crazy woman walked into his office in a raincoat and nothing else. He'd told her the ploy was pathetically cliché. She'd offered to suck him off under his desk and unfortunately, he'd let her. Since then she'd become clingy, and that was when Cory made his rule: no serial dating. Actually it was no serial fucking, sucking, dry humping, or any other form of passion that led to climax.

Since he'd been engaging in casual sex with so many other women, Amanda had cooled her jets.

Cory walked into the examination room where the young woman and dog were waiting. She was seated in the only chair in the room, rocking the Airedale.

Her luminous large green eyes looked up to him. "He needs to be euthanized. His usual vet was closed for the day. Please help me."

Cory knelt in front of the woman and petted the dog. "What's his name?"

"Randy."

"Hey, Randy," Cory said as he stroked the dog's head. Randy raised his eyelids and looked to Cory. Then he closed his eyes and winced. Cory saw the large tumor between his legs. Given its size, Cory guessed it must be interwoven into Randy's internal organs.

His owner was crying silently, tears streaking down her lightly freckled face.

"I can offer pain management, but I assume he's on medication already."

She nodded, her eyes fixed to the floor. "The meds were managing his pain until today."

"He's old."

She nodded again, her head lightly resting on the dog. "Seventeen."

"That's a full life for a dog. Damned good life. If you want to say goodbye, I can give you some time, and then I'll take him."

"No!" Her head rose as her brows slanted inward and her eyes grew wide. "I want to hold him when you do it." She kissed Randy. "I need to hold him."

Cory's head tilted as he studied her. "Uh, I don't think that's a good idea."

She squeezed her eyes shut and bowed her head. Her long chestnut hair, with copper highlights that sparkled under the florescent lights of the exam room, hid her face.

"You don't understand. Randy has been there for me. Always. He's the only remaining link between my parents and me. He was our family dog. We got him when I was seven." She stroked the dog's back. "I can't let him go out alone. I'll be here with him."

He'd seen this woman around his brother's brewery. She worked there on weekends, but kept to herself. She wasn't like the other women who worked there, definitely not like the one who'd actually groped him under the table; he'd had her in the bathroom. Had never even gotten her name.

The chestnut-haired beauty's distress weighed on him. And not only because her body heat reached out to him when he crouched in front of her. "I've seen you around. You work at The Good Doctor."

"Yes." Her head rested on Randy's as she continued to rock him.

"I didn't get your name."

"Brook Walker."

"Brook Walker." Cory's eyes turned wide as he recalled what he'd read about her in the Whisky Cove Herald. "The Brook Walker that rescues greyhounds from the race park?"

She nodded. "That's me."

Cory's mouth opened on a whispered "Wow." His gaze fixed on her. She'd rescued dozens of dogs and found them homes with people deemed suitable owners of a rescue greyhound. "You train them to be companion dogs, don't you?"

She nodded again, and this time a strangled cry broke from her lips.

It was killing him to see her like that, so he scooped Randy into his arms. "Come with me."

Brook was on her feet quickly. "What are you doing?" she demanded.

"I'm taking you and Randy out to my home, where there are stables and where we can all get comfortable, especially Randy."

Her brows furrowed as she shook her head. "What? Your home? I don't need you to do that; I just need him euthanized. Will you do it or not?"

Cory stopped at the door when it was clear she wasn't going to follow. "I can do that here on the stainless steel." He indicated the exam table with his head. "Or at a stable where we could lay him down on a bale of hay and let you take your time with him." Cory's body tensed. "Er, there's also the matter of the burial."

Her head cocked. "The burial?"

"Well, if you leave him here, he'll be cremated. It's the law."

She sucked in a quick breath.

"If you prefer a more peaceful resting place, there's a pecan grove at my childhood home. You could visit whenever you like."

She nodded as she thought through his words. "If it's not an imposition, I would greatly appreciate the pecan grove."

Cory tilted his head. "Don't mention it. It's the least I can do. After all, you put up with Logan at the brewery week after week." He walked her out to his SUV and motioned for her to open the rear door. He laid Randy gently on the seat, on an old blanket already lying there. He handed her the keys so that she could start the ignition. "Just let me grab a few things we'll need, and I'll be right back." She offered a tight smile this time with her nod.

As Cory was making his way back inside, her smile went with him. He thought of her full lips and the pretty white teeth that peeked through. He'd like to taste those lips. He grabbed the things he would need to put Randy in eternal sleep. He took a deep breath and released it slowly. He knew what Brook was feeling. He would do his best to make Randy's last moments as painless as possible for her.

Cory and Brook arrived at the gates of the St. Martin estate twenty minutes later. His father was in Lake Charles on business, so they would have the run of the place. Maybe he would grill some shrimp for them, if she felt like eating. She sat in the back on the ride over and murmured to Randy, words that Cory couldn't make out from the driver's seat. She truly was alone. He'd asked about her parents and discovered they'd both died. The story she'd shared about their deaths had reached out and grabbed him by the throat. He was determined to help her through the difficult night she had ahead of her.

Cory drove straight to the stables. He looked into the rearview mirror at Brook's red face, at the tears falling steadily. He parked in front of the stables and shifted to face her. He'd learned that no matter how painful, it was best to come clean regarding the events to come. Knowledge made things easier in the long run. "I suggest we get set up in the stables and, when you're ready, I'll administer the drugs." She was back to silently nodding.

Cory opened the rear door and removed Randy from her lap. Brook followed him into the stables. "Grab that blanket from the wall, will you?" Brook immediately complied. "Drape it across the bed of hay." Cory tried hard to not disturb the resting dog but when he laid him on the blanket, Randy opened his eyes and moaned. "There you are, old boy." Brook took the spot beside her dog.

Cory returned to his SUV for the black bag that held the drugs that would take Randy out of this world. The dog needed to be put down, but he knew it would be hard on Brook and he hated that she would forever connect him to her pain. He'd put down several animals since he'd opened his vet practice. Of course the owners grieved but they all did it differently. He wondered how Brook would do it. Usually, there were two grievers, two owners. Would Cory need to comfort her? The thought wasn't unpleasant to him, which he found odd. He shrugged.

Cory was glad the horses they usually kept were currently housed at his practice for breeding; they had the stable to themselves. He walked in and sat opposite Brook, leaving the dog between them. "I know you're aware that Randy is in a lot of pain. You're doing the right thing."

Brook's anguished green eyes met his. "Please, I'm ready."

Cory didn't say a word. He pulled the loaded syringes from his black bag and took Randy's paw into his hand and did what needed to be done.

Randy would be in a state of eternal sleep soon. His respiration was slowing.

Brook put her lips to his ear and said, "I love you, Randy. I'll miss you."

Cory wanted to give them privacy but when he rose to his feet, Brook grabbed his ankle.

He looked down and watched the tension ease from her tight shoulders on a deep exhalation of air.

"Will you stay here with me? Please. I don't have anyone else." Her lips trembled, and her sorrow filled the stable.

Cory wanted to comfort her, but he didn't know her, didn't know what she'd need. He lowered himself to the ground and sat quietly with her. Brook pulled Randy tight against her and leaned into Cory. His body immediately went rigid. He wasn't used to this kind of intimacy with women. Brook held Randy and lodged her head under Cory's chin. His body responded naturally. Without thinking, he snaked his arm around her waist. Her hair, smelling of wildflowers, tickled his nose and. Her bronze skin glistened in the glow of the overhead lights. Cory suddenly, urgently, wanted to taste that skin but he willed his desire down. The last thing she needed was Cory preying on her as though she were an animal in heat.

They sat quietly for about fifteen minutes. Rigor mortis would soon set in, and Cory didn't want Brook hugging Randy when it did. She hadn't moved since he'd placed his arm around her waist. To avoid startling her, he spoke softly into her ear. "I think we should talk about what you want to do next."

She turned her head to meet his eyes. "You mentioned a pecan grove?"

Cory smiled. "Yes, I think Randy would like it there; it's my favorite part of the property. Do you want to take him there now?"

Brook turned to look at the lifeless dog that lay across her lap. She whispered, "Okay."

Cory stood. "Let me get Randy, and you can help me gather some tools." He immediately loaded Randy into the Mule 4x4 and used a blanket to cover him.

He walked back in and directed Brook, just to give her something to focus on.

"Get the rake and the lanterns from that table." Cory motioned toward the table, and he turned to grab the shovel. He hoisted a bag of sodium hydroxide onto his shoulder. "And take a couple of those gray blankets from the shelf behind the table too." They loaded all the items into the

Mule and Cory drove to the garage. "I'm just gonna get some water." He leaped from the Mule.

Leaning against the refrigerator was a spear with white ribbon dangling from the tip. Cory snagged the stick to mark Randy's grave.

He drove them to the back part of the property and unloaded the tools. He should have changed clothes, but he hadn't wanted to leave Brook alone with her thoughts and her dead dog. It was hot, so he loosened his tie and removed it. His shirt followed. He started on the job of digging Randy's grave.

CHAPTER 2

Brook couldn't believe the selflessness of this man. She'd walked into the first clinic she came to after discovering her vet's office was closed. She'd heard Cory was a womanizer and in general a pig toward women, had in fact witnessed his poor behavior on two separate occasions herself. So his sensitivity with her didn't add up. He seemed to genuinely care about her and her dog.

Bronzed brawny muscle rippled across his shoulders and chest as he used the shovel to dig Randy's grave. Whenever he jumped onto the shovel, digging deep into the ground, his trousers slid down to reveal a little more abdominal—and have mercy—more pelvic muscle. Brook watched in full euphoric bliss as moisture flooded her core. The man was any woman's dream. For a moment Brook forgot about Randy. It was a welcome change.

Looking out across the acres of St. Martin land, Brook wondered what it must have been like to grow up with such beauty. The abundance of land was a luxury that would have given Cory a childhood like no other. He would have spent countless lazy summer days out here without a care. She smiled when she thought of him as a dusty-headed child climbing trees and wreaking havoc on any reptile or little girl who crossed his path. He had six siblings, including Logan, so Cory would never have been alone, as she was now.

Manly grunts drew her back to the task at hand. She continued to watch Cory. Once the hole was large enough, Cory gently lowered Randy into his eternal place of rest. He was wrapped in a blanket. Cory looked to Brook and asked, "Do you want to say anything?"

Brook squatted down and placed her hand on Randy's stiff body. "I love you, D." She stood and nodded to Cory. He opened a bag of white powder and poured it over the blanket that enveloped Randy and then covered him with dirt. Once the hole was filled, Cory retrieved a wooden post with a white ribbon from the 4x4. He used a hammer to drive it into the ground.

Brook stood frozen as she thanked God for the kindness of this man. He'd taken her bad situation and made it bearable. She'd felt utterly hopeless when she'd walked through the clinic doors. If she'd had to go home alone after putting Randy down in an impersonal manner, she would have been in a deep depression for days. Instead she was hopeful as she stood next to Randy's marker with the white ribbon. Hopeful and pleased that she would have a place to visit. For that she would always be thankful for Dr. Corrigan St. Martin.

The last time she'd experienced the love of family was when she was nine. That was the year her parents died. She'd longed for a companion, a sister or brother she could confide in. She'd almost gotten her wish. It had been so close. If she closed her eyes she could picture her mother's large round belly. She had been two weeks past due. They'd all been so excited about the baby. They'd been the three musketeers, but were ready for a fourth.

Brook had been in a science class, happily messing with test tubes and colored liquids, when they came for her. It was midmorning. Her parents had died in a car wreck—dead on impact. She'd been sent to the East Coast to live with her uncle and his wife, a couple she'd never met. She wished she could still claim that pleasure. She shook off a shudder, turning her attention back to Cory. He was making the burial site neat, making sure, she knew, that animals wouldn't dig into it.

She'd moved back to Whisky Cove as an adult because it was where she'd lived with her parents. It was the last place she'd been happy. She'd hoped to find happiness again in the little town, and so far it hadn't disappointed her. The town was a good base for her dog rescues. By next week she'd have a full house. Yet if she had the space, she could do so much more. She looked over the sweep of land in front of her. She could do a lot with a place like this. Her mind replayed the image of the stable. Yes, plenty of space for animals, though she hadn't seen any horses in the large space. Maybe the St. Martin's didn't have any these days. But Cory was a veterinarian. Surely he could see the necessity of letting her stable some rescue animals. She'd figure out a way to work her idea into a conversation.

Cory loaded the tools back into the 4x4. Then he pulled out a bottle of water, and Brook stared, dazed, as he tilted his head back and drank it down in three large gulps. He looked like a model from a TV commercial, hired for his physical perfection. His bronzed muscular chest and torso were made more prominent by his provocative posture. Water or sweat, or a mixture, sluiced down his chest between his pectorals. Brook's tongue swept her top lip as she inhaled steady and deep.

Cory's head popped back up, but she was too slow to put on a neutral face. The right side of his lip quirked in a sexy smirk, and a lone brow rose, indicating he'd caught her watching and didn't mind that she did. Brook pivoted and stared into the pecan grove. She heard Cory laugh. He joined her and offered her a bottle of water.

Heavy drops of moisture landed on her arms, and without warning a deluge dumped on them. Brook was soaked through in seconds. She turned her face toward the heavens and let the rain wash away her sadness. Cory joined her, turning his face to the sky.

When the lightning and thunder started, Cory said, "We're miles away from the house." He looked at the 4x4 and out across the land. He grabbed blankets and a lantern from the vehicle. "Follow me." He led them into a thicket of pecan trees and didn't stop moving until they stood before a tall structure that resembled a beach house. It was all wood and perched high above the ground on stilts. A porch and windows wrapped around the sides.

"What is it?"

"Deer stand. We'll be safe here; it's outfitted with a lightning rod." He pointed to the stairs. "Climb."

Some fancy deer stand. Brook guessed that the St. Martin boys had done a lot of playing in it when they were young.

When she reached the top, Cory reached around her and opened the door. Her canvas shoes were soaked and rubbed her heel, so she toed them off by the door as she took in the deer stand. The inside was not as fancy as the outside—just unfinished plywood walls and floors, and an old couch the sole piece of furniture in the large space.

His body was soaked and so was hers. Cory stood shirtless, with the weight of the water drawing his pants low enough that Brook got a look at the thin trail of light brown hair that started under his navel and ran narrowly down his veined and muscular lower abs, leading into his trousers. She swallowed down the lump in her throat, which had her focusing on her breathing; it was erratic. But she couldn't control it. And she couldn't draw her eyes away from the bewitching vision before her. He was the most perfect male specimen she'd ever seen.

When her gaze found his eyes, the realization that he was focused on her chest caused her senses to go haywire. Her nipples hardened, feeling tight and achy. She looked down to see them poking at her T-shirt. She instinctively crossed her arms to shield them from his view.

Dilated dark eyes stared at her. Brook couldn't look away. His heated eyes seemed to be circled by a glowing ice ring, and she didn't know if she wanted to shiver or melt.

He cleared his throat.

"So you work at the brewery on weekends."

As she thought of her job at the brewery, she recalled his amorous activities the last night she had been there. She nodded and narrowed her eyes at him.

"Why are you looking at me like that?"

She attempted to flatten out her features. "Like what?"

"Like I'm a snake."

She shrugged and looked down as she traced designs on the floor with her toe. "I saw you in the bathroom." She paused her tracing and threw him a glance. "Having sex with Lucy."

His eyes grew large as he gasped. "Shit! I knew someone had opened the door, but my back was to it and the woman I was with . . ."

"Lucy? The one who told me to F-off?"

His hand rubbed the back of his neck. "God, it was you." He shook his head, then muttered, "Why the hell did it have to be you?"

She blushed. "I needed to use the bathroom. You should have locked the door."

He tilted his head and audibly exhaled. "You should have knocked."

Brook's eyes met his, and she lifted her brow.

"What? Why are you always glaring at me?"

She plucked an imaginary piece of lint from her shorts. "I'm not glaring."

"You are so glaring."

"Were you having sex with your client in the exam room before you saw me?"

His eyes grew wide. He choked off the breath he was inhaling. "How did you know?"

"A combination of factors." She counted them off on her fingers. "The repetitive noises for one. You were also straightening your tie when you opened the door. And Mrs. Simms was patting herself down, preening in a post-coital glow."

"Uh, you know her?"

"Her husband is one of my regular customers. I actually bought my home from him—rent to own. If it weren't for him, I wouldn't have a home of my own."

"You're judging me then."

She held up her hands in denial. "Not judging."

"Then what is it you're doing? Why even ask about it? Why even tell me about her husband? Are you jealous?" His voice was defensive and loud.

Her head jerked up. His hands were clenched at his sides.

"I believe you should have all the facts," he told her.

Brook stared unwaveringly into his eyes. Right, he was going to tell her why everything he did was okay. She prepared herself for his version of the guilty man's lament.

"Evidently he's not fucking her well enough at home. We are both consenting adults. It's not my business why she seeks sex outside of her marriage. Besides, if she didn't do me, she'd just get it somewhere else."

Brook gasped and her body went numb. Not only was he adulterer, but also he was shameless about his behavior. It didn't add up—he was two distinct versions of himself. The animal loving, caring man and the careless, shameless adulterer.

"You know I'm fucking right!"

Brooks hands covered her ears. "Will you please stop shouting and using that word."

He whispered, making fun of her, no doubt, "You certainly are self-righteous."

He stomped out and slammed the door, causing the shelter to rattle around her. A chill raced down Brook's spine. This was a different man from the one she'd experienced earlier. Where he'd been gentle and caring, now he was aggressive and on the defensive. She wondered how such vibrant personalities lived in one person. Mostly she wondered why he acted the way he did with women.

She stepped to the window and watched him head toward the 4x4. Her scalp tingled as she looked out across the landscape. A muffled crackle broke through the dark clouds hovering above, and a whisker of energy grew into a grand display as she watched. Frantically leaning into the glass, she searched for Cory and saw him crouch on the ground. He shouted, "Shit!" and then raced back toward the shelter. Brook listened to him scramble up the ladder, and then he slammed open the door and stepped inside.

Brook ran to him. "Oh my God." She ran her hands over his chest and face. "Are you okay?"

He grasped her hands firmly, halting her actions—his gaze hot on her. "What are you doing?"

The heat and heavy breath from his mouth landed on her cheeks.

Brook tugged her hands, but he wouldn't release them. He didn't even blink, but his chest rose and fell unsteadily. Intense heat radiated from his body and reached toward hers.

"I'm sorry about your friend," he said. "It's not a good excuse, but I really didn't know." He looked down at their entwined hands. "Look, I'll make it my mission to obtain facts first. Fact number one will be marital status. Okay?"

Brook nodded. "Okay." He didn't owe her anything. The fact that he was willing to make a change because of her, because of a passing look, did funny things to her insides. He headed to the couch, pulling her with him. They sat on opposite ends.

Cory lit a lantern. "Are you cold?"

Even though the temperatures were mild, Brook's wet clothes were chilling her. Cory shook out a blanket and tossed it over her lower half. They sat listening to the storm. A booming thunderclap landed near the shelter, shaking the building and rattling the window. It was so loud Brook's head vibrated. She screamed and when Cory held his arms open, she scampered into his lap and buried her face in his chest.

Given her nose was at the level of his neck, and therefore at a pulse point, Cory's scent was strong. Smells of leather, hay, and sweaty male hit her senses and caused her libido to tingle. His scent drew her in like a bee to pollen. Her nose pressed to his skin, and she inhaled deeply. Then she just naturally nuzzled at his neck. His pulse against her lips had her imagining what it would be like to graze her teeth against the vein in his neck. A husky growl sounded from him, from deep within his throat. That was when Brook realized she'd acted on her thought.

Head lowered in embarrassment, she whispered, "I can't believe I just did that. I'm sorry."

With his finger under her chin, Cory raised her head. "Hey, will you do something for me?"

His eyes were constricted orbs of smoked steel. They were mesmerizing. She nodded.

"Shut off your mind and listen to your desire."

Brook knew that listening to his deep-voiced suggestion rather than the ever quieter voice of reason was probably a mistake, but her need for him was as fierce as it was sudden. She needed to be held, needed to be passionate with someone. She wanted to feel life, and Cory St. Martin was vividly alive. Her body yearned for him. Desire fueled the fire in her sex, and her mind switched allegiances, wanting to please her body rather than rigid rules.

His palms went to her cheeks, and her body trembled. He pressed his lips to hers, kissing with light pressure. He pulled up and whispered against her moistened lips, "Sweet."

She was nervous, but she did what she'd wanted to do since she got her first glimpse of his bare chest. She stretched her fingers out and ran the tips of them down the muscles of his pecs. Her mouth opened on a sigh. She could definitely understand the temptation of Cory St. Martin, of wanting to be bedded by him. His body and his smile promised pleasure beyond the norm. In his presence she'd gone from a girl who never gave sex much thought to a woman aching for a man's sensual touch. Aching for this man's touch. She hoped he would hurry and make his move because if he didn't, she was about to beg him to take her.

***

When Cory looked down and saw hard nipples through her thin cotton shirt, the sight had him instantly hard. He'd been sporting a semi ever since she'd snuggled up to him in the stables, so he hadn't had far to go. He didn't understand it. He'd stroked himself to release that morning in the shower and then he'd had Mrs. Simms. Usually after two bouts, he was good for the day.

She seemed to be exploring him as if he were a surprise to her, as if his body fascinated her. Her fingertips on his skin sparked, branding him and scarring where she touched. When she pressed closer and nuzzled into his neck, he knew he was in trouble. She traced those luscious lips higher up his neck. At his chin, she rubbed back and forth. He stopped her long enough to lower them to the floor, then he leaned his back against the couch. He took her bottom lip into his mouth and savored it, stroking again and again. He groaned when he tasted cherry. He guessed it was her lipstick. Whatever it was, it was heady and drove him wild. She climbed atop him and straddled him. They rubbed into one another. When her lips parted on a moan, Cory used the opportunity to press his tongue inside. God, she tasted like heaven. He ravaged her mouth, exploring and tasting and taking. When they broke apart, both breathing hard, their eyes met. Her luminous green had turned a dark olive. The gold flecks in them seemed to be sparkling in the low light slanting into the deer stand.

Cory knew he shouldn't take advantage of her grief, but God, her desire had turned her into a temptress, one he wasn't able to resist. He wasn't going to tell her this, but a woman's reaction to him was the reason he had so much sex. He knew what the heated looks meant. He enjoyed being wanted and needed. By far, Brook's reaction was the most erotic he'd ever experienced. He'd never seen a woman burn so hotly. Her response made his cock ache.

Cory pulled her shirt over her head to reveal a tiny athletic figure. She was lean, with a muscular body. It wasn't the kind of muscle that made her look masculine but the kind that made everything tight. She was thin but also feminine and graceful. He couldn't wait to sink his teeth into her body.

Brook's firm little breasts glinted with droplets of water from his hair, and Cory bent to lick them away. She tasted of honey and smelled of lavender. While he lapped the drops from her body, Cory unclasped her bra and slid it free. She had just enough flesh to fill his palm. Cory liked that size—not too big, not too small, just right. Before he could do more than admire them, Brook stood and slid her cutoff shorts down her wet thighs. Her white silk panties were soaked and practically translucent. He could clearly see the folds of her pussy. His fingers landed on that spot, and he slid them over the wet silk. Brook's mouth opened on a gasp. His mouth watered at the sight of her cunt just in front of his lips. He yearned to taste her, to devour her. He slid her wet panties down and plunged his index and middle fingers through the lips of her sex. And then it was clear to him that she wasn't wet just from the rainwater. He pushed one finger as deep as he could. She choked around his name. He pulled his fingers free, and her blazing eyes watched as he cleaned them with his mouth.

Brook knelt in front of him, unbuckled his belt, and pulled down his zipper. She reached inside the waistband of his boxers and pulled him free. Her eyes dilated.

Cory smirked at her. "Do you like what you see?"

A breathy moan released from her throat. "It's um . . . " She cleared her throat.

"It's what?"

"It's long and thick and bulbous."

Cory laughed. He'd never been called bulbous. Long and thick, yes. Bulbous, no. She stroked him even as she knelt between his thighs and took him in her mouth. She used her tongue to massage the underside of his shaft while she sucked him into her warm, wet heat. She only managed to accommodate half his size before reversing her path.

Cory's hands slid into her silky hair. Brook plunged her mouth down half his length. When she pulled back, Cory held her head in place. He whispered, "Brook, you can take more." With a thrust of his hips, he pushed his cock into her mouth. When he felt Brook's throat relax, he pushed home. He fucked her mouth until he was coming down the back of her throat. Brook took every last drop of him and swallowed it down. Cory groaned, "God, I love your mouth."

He slowly pulled his penis free, not wanting to leave the warmth. Brook lowered her head and eyes, and bit her bottom lip. God, it was seduction itself. She sat with her butt on the rough wooden floor of the shelter and pulled her knees up to her chest, never once taking her eyes off him.

"Where do you think you're going?" he asked. "I'm not done with you yet."

He pulled her toward him and laid her across the pallet he'd made out of the blankets. He hiked her knees up toward her chest so that her core was fully exposed to him. "Don't move." He kissed the inside of her thigh and then moved to the other one and did the same. She giggled, but the sound was low and arousing. He hovered over her heated channel for the longest time, inhaling deep. A rosy blush spread across her body.

Cory rubbed his nose through her sex. She smelled like the fresh cream his grandmother used to churn in the barn. He remembered smearing that fresh butter over a roll fresh from the oven and sinking his teeth into it. Suddenly he realized he was starving, that a feast lay before him, and he immediately tasted her mound. She cried out his name. He hoped that meant she liked what he was doing, because he didn't intend to stop. He massaged her clit with his thumb and fucked her with his tongue. Within seconds she was writhing against his mouth. Within minutes she was coming, her release making him grin, making him hard again.

Once Cory drew the last of her juices from her, he moved to his knees and positioned his anxiously waiting cock in front of her opening. He didn't have any condoms on him since his wallet was in the glove box of his SUV, but he had to have her. Using his hand to guide him to her entrance, he plunged the full length of himself into her soft liquid heat. The move elicited a deep low moan from the back of Brook's throat, and she exhaled on a gasp. She went still.

"Am I hurting you?" he asked.

"Mmm, no, I'm just intensely . . . wonderfully full at the moment."

Cory knew what that meant and held himself as still as possible while she adjusted to accept him. Not thrusting was hard, however, because her entire body was quivering beneath him, calling to him and turning him on so hard that he started shaking in reaction. The whole cycle of it was a new sensation he'd not experienced before, and it had his body sizzling to the core. He thought he could feel her pulse at the head of his penis, and his erection grew inside her. He needed to move—God, he needed to move—but she just lay there, quivering and pulsing beneath him.

"Brook, are you sure you're okay?"

"Yes. I need you to ride me long and hard."

Goddamn. Here was a woman who knew exactly what she wanted. Cory looked at her laid open before him and thought about how to get the best leverage to meet her demands. He rose up on spread knees. "Slide your legs around my waist."

As soon as she crossed her ankles behind his back, he was able to go in an inch deeper. Her chest rose and fell in a shallow rhythm. He clasped his hands around the small of her back to arch her toward him. Her head fell back, and a low groan vibrated through her chest. Her hands wrapped around his wrists as her chest bowed. Her small round tits stood at attention and seemed like they were reaching up to kiss the sky. He moved, using a firm hold to give it to her hard. On every upward thrust he pulled her down violently onto his shaft. Her lips maintained a low murmur of rapture. Cory pounded so forcefully, her small tight breasts were dancing with every thrust. He drove her like a truck as he pushed her all the way to a final state of abandon. She climaxed on a hoarse whisper of his name, and he used one hand to firmly pinch each of her fully engorged nipples. With each wave that pulsed through her, she squeezed his dick tighter and harder until he was emptying into her. She drew his come from him as though she was milking him, unwilling to leave even one drop. He hadn't intended to spill inside of her but as tight as she was, he didn't think he could have pulled out had he wanted to. And he hadn't wanted to.

Cory was reluctant to leave her warmth. He turned them until they could spoon, and they remained connected. He pulled the blanket over their bodies, and they slept, riding out the storm.

CHAPTER 3

The manic twitter of birds chirping and the light filtering in through the windows had Cory slowly coming awake. In his half-awakened state, he sensed his hardening shaft being squeezed. Shit. He was mortified that he was whacking off with Brook right next to him. He enjoyed the embarrassing pleasure for a moment longer, until he realized that it was Brook's hot cunt and not his hand that was squeezing his cock. And then he groaned.

He guessed it was his hard thickness invading her body that had Brook awakening on a gasp. God, he'd fallen asleep pressed inside her, and they'd stayed that way all night. Brook looked over her shoulder as he pulled himself free from her channel. "Shit. Sorry about that." This had become way too intimate for his blood.

He rolled to his back and exhaled heavily. What were they doing?

Brook rolled to her back as well, and Cory lifted his wrist to check his watch just to have something to do.

"Damn!" He sat up. "I'm late for an appointment." He was supposed to be over at the Miller's farm to check on and possibly deliver their prized Holstein.

Brook sat up and then stood to pull on her clothes. Cory stood as well and immediately hit his head on a wooden beam, forgetting he was a lot taller than when he was a child. "Dammit!"

He dressed while Brook gathered up the lantern and blankets. She climbed down the stairs of the deer stand, Cory following after her. "Where can I drop you?"

"I don't live far from your practice."

"Sounds good."

They walked to the 4x4 in silence. He was cursing himself for having had unprotected sex with her. Where the hell had his mind been?

He grunted, knowing very well where it had been—balls deep in Brook's pussy. He wondered if she was going to get clingy or angry or start to pout. He turned to look at her, but she was smiling wide as she inhaled deeply and took in her surroundings.

He caught her eye, and she said, "It's beautiful out here."

Cory grumbled as he wondered if she was always this chipper in the morning.

"I wanted to thank you for yesterday."

His legs froze. He narrowed his eyes on her. Where was she headed?

She shrugged and focused her gaze on his shoulder. "If you hadn't been available to help me with Randy, I don't know what I would have done. When I think of him buried here surrounded by all this peacefulness, it makes me happy."

He grumbled again. For a minute there he'd thought she was thanking him for sex. His gut had clenched. He hoped she wouldn't even bring it up but if she did, he hoped she understood it wouldn't happen again. What he'd done with her was careless and irresponsible.

When they reached the 4x4, he was relieved. The sooner he got her where she needed to be and away from him, the sooner he could focus. He couldn't think straight around her. He didn't understand it, but he thought his reaction might have to do with the intensity of the sex. When Brook had been slithering around him, he'd felt her quivers and her fevered skin penetrate his boundaries, the walls he used to keep women and their emotions at bay. He'd heard of out of body experiences, and he thought maybe they'd shared one.

A scary thought.

There was a moment he thought she'd stopped breathing, had imagined her heart had stopped beating. It was when she'd climaxed around him. Then he'd realized that her breath and heart rhythms had changed to match his own. Once she'd fallen asleep, he'd watched her chest rise and fall and felt her heart's steady beat with his palm to her chest. The pattern never veered from his, even when he'd tried to force it by holding his breath. It was like they had died and been reborn as one. It spooked the hell out of him, yet he'd held onto her throughout the night, worried about what would happen if he let go.

He turned the key on the 4x4, but the engine didn't turn over. He smashed his palm into the steering wheel with force. "Fuck!"

Brook's eyes widened at him.

"Er, sorry." Great, now he was apologizing.

Dammit, hadn't he told Cash to install a new battery? With the exception of Cash, all the brothers used the ranch regularly, but since Cory lived there, he got stuck tending to the chores unless he forced the others to do something. "We're gonna have to walk back to the house." He circled around to grab rubber boots out of the back for her to wear. "Here, put these on. Some of the land is cleared, but some is wooded." He stomped away before she had a chance to pull on the boots. His hope was that she would keep that distance, but no such luck. She maintained a light jog to match the pace of his long stride. When she stumbled over a root, he felt like an ass. He braced her so she wouldn't fall and then he slowed his strides.

Green eyes sparkled at him. "There's a lot of land here. Do you put it to use?"

"We use it for the horses."

"I haven't seen any horses."

"We have two prized stallions. They're at my clinic now, but they're usually out here."

"Two horses." She nodded as she looked out across the lush rolling landscape. Her gaze landed on Cory's, and her brows rose.

What the hell? She was a scheming little thing. Cory shrugged in an exaggerated gesture. "What?"

"Well." She tilted her chin back and used her fingernails to lightly stroke her neck. "You've got a lot of land here. Have you ever considered using it for charity?"

Cory stopped, shocked. "Charity!"

"Yeah." She smiled as she looked left to right, sweeping her arm out with her gaze. "I could do so much with the dogs here."

Cory stuffed his hands into his pockets and kicked a rock. What the hell was happening? Was she trying to ingratiate herself with him? "I don't know, it can be dangerous out here."

She nodded. "I gotcha." Some of the fire went out of her eyes, but she held on to her smile.

Shit. He wanted to see her eyes blaze. He supposed it couldn't hurt to let her use an acre or two during the day to train her dogs. Hell, most days he didn't even get home until after six. By then she'd be long gone. He shrugged. "I guess it would be okay if you wanted to bring your dogs here for training, but you'll need to be gone by five."

Her eyes flared to life and a gorgeous large smile of sparkling white teeth erupted across her face. It warmed him, and not only in a sexual way, and he knew he would agree to anything to see that smile. Damn, he was royally fucked.

She skipped ahead of him and turned to grasp his hands. Her hair flowed like field grasses in the wind. He couldn't help smiling.

"Think of the karma you'll reap."

What? She was certifiable. Cory frowned. "Karma?"

"By giving so generously to the animal community, you'll probably become the next Dr. Doolittle." She dropped his hands and held her palm out to him. "Here's to a new and exciting collaboration."

Her eyes danced. What was behind the expression, he didn't know. He hoped it wasn't something that would bite him in the ass. But what the hell? How bad could it be? He could always tell her to leave if the arrangement didn't work out. He placed his palm in her hand and was shocked by the surge of energy that sparked from her skin to his.

***

At the Miller's farm the Holstein was birthed without a hitch. Cory went home to clean up and shower and was now on his way to his practice. When he arrived he saw that one of his clients was due to bring in a litter of Airedale terriers for third-round shots. And that had him thinking about Brook and her loss. All morning, green eyes and chestnut hair interrupted his thoughts. Every time he washed up with the green hand soap in the exam room, he saw her eyes. When he went to check on Ambassador, one of his father's horses, he imagined the horse's hair to be the exact same rich color as Brook's.

Christ, he was losing it.

When the owner of the terrier pups came in, Cory asked him if he was ready to sell. To Cory's delight, the man was. When Cory asked how much he wanted, the owner quoted twelve hundred dollars. Cory had expected as much—they were beauties. But he offered one thousand cash for one of the males. His client bartered for some premium dog food, and Cory conceded. He acquired a little brown and black rascal on the spot. He called him Teddy because the little guy looked like a traditional teddy bear.

After work he collected the pup and pulled a small collar off a shelf. He also made up a bag with dog food and other items he thought Teddy might need. He pulled up outside Brook's house at six thirty.

His knocks went unanswered. Cory was resigned to taking Teddy home with him when he heard a whistle coming from the backyard. He walked around the house and from the back gate he watched Brook working with one of her rescue greyhounds.

She was teaching the dog to stay and retrieve. Making use of hand gestures and her voice, she commanded the greyhound to stay as she squeaked a toy and threw it. When the dog started to get up, she reinforced the command with a gesture and a short blow of a whistle. The dog was intently focused on her as she praised him. When she said, "Go, Eagle," he flew across the small yard to retrieve the toy. She knelt, and the dog brought her the toy. She laughed as he nudged her and licked her face.

"What a smart boy you are."

When she turned her head, their eyes met and Cory was aware he had a dumb smile on his face, one that probably revealed way too much. He opened the gate, and Eagle immediately sat at a statuesque attention, leaning into Brook's leg. She petted him in encouragement and, through unspoken language, Brook conveyed her acceptance of Cory to the dog. As Brook scratched between the dog's ears, Cory wished he was leaning against her leg as she caressed him. He was in awe as he watched the connection she had with the dog. She made it look easy when he knew it was anything but. Rescue dogs didn't act like other dogs. Destructive behaviors and aggressive tendencies could prevent a bond from developing between master and canine. Counterconditioning could take months. Good handlers could get to the bottom of irrational fears, bad habits, and trust issues, but it took consistent routines and clear expectations of boundaries. Most people gave up on the dogs long before any routine could be established.

Observing Brook with the dog was humbling. Clearly she'd earned Eagle's trust, and now he looked to her for guidance on how to process the intruder. She comforted his anxiety and put him at ease. She used facial gestures, body movements, and sounds to communicate with the animal. Theirs was an innate, primal connection reminiscent of a friendship in a past life.

Eagle saw her as the leader of his pack. That acceptance had no doubt taken some skill, and Cory was in awe as to how the small chestnut-haired woman with the large smile and scattering of freckles had managed it.

Once Eagle had been put at ease, Cory walked toward them. When Brook saw the sleeping puppy in Cory's arms, she cupped her cheeks in her hands. Her eyes filled with liquid, she gasped, "Wherever did you find him?"

Cory smiled and removed his sunglasses. "One of my clients is a breeder." He held Teddy like a championship trophy and said, "Say hello to your new pup."

Brook started to cry, and Cory froze. That wasn't the reaction he'd wanted. He'd pictured one of those smiles that showcased her beautiful teeth. Eagle started moving, getting antsy as he sensed Brook's emotions.

"Can I hold him?" Brook asked.

Cory offered a tight, worried smile, "Well, of course. Teddy's yours after all." He didn't know what he'd do if she continued to be all emotional.

Brook held out her hands, and Cory delicately passed Teddy to her. She studied him and then kissed the top of his head.

"You are a sweetie, yes you are." Holding the puppy, Brook knelt in front of Eagle. He suspiciously sniffed the unfamiliar animal. Her voice low and hoarse, Brook said, "Look, Eagle, it's a new brother for you. He's sweet, isn't he?" Eagle licked Teddy's snout. "We like him, don't we?" Eagle licked her face. It seemed the little pup would fit in well.

She stood and smiled at Cory. "Thank you. What do I owe you?"

"Nothing."

Her brow rose as she looked down to the dog in her arms. She stroked him. "That's not true. He's super-coated and you got him from a breeder; I'm sure you paid dearly. How much?"

"Brook, I bought him for you because I wanted you to have him. I won't accept any money." He didn't want to talk about money. As he looked around her yard and took in the torn window screens and crumbled steps on the house, he wondered if she even had enough.

Brook held the pup up in front of her face. "Well, this little guy is very sweet and very special. You come visit whenever you want. Did I hear you call him Teddy?"

"Yeah, but feel free to call him whatever you like. That was just something I came up with today."

"I think it's a perfect name—St. Martin's Teddy Bear." Brook touched the pup's nose to hers. "If you won't let me pay you, then you must join us for dinner."

"Us? Is someone here?"

"I meant me, Eagle, and Teddy."

"You cook for Eagle, do you?"

"Actually, we're having spaghetti tonight."

"I like spaghetti."

Cory was curious to see inside her house, and dinner would give him the perfect opportunity to scope it out.

She walked ahead of him and motioned for him to follow. Eagle walked at her side, but he kept an eye on Cory.

Inside the house, Brook handed Teddy off to Cory. He pulled the bag from his shoulder and tended to the pup. He'd even brought a bed. Most young pups slept the majority of the day, so they needed a cozy and comforting place to sleep. Cory set him up in the corner of the kitchen that shared a wall with the living room, and every now and then Teddy would open his eyes and lift his head to look around.

Brook's house was built in a late nineteenth-century shotgun style. It had been updated sometime, but clearly not recently. The kitchen sink leaked and rust stained the basin. Tiles in the countertop were loose and some were missing all together. Looking at the modest surroundings, he was curious how much income Brook had. He assumed her work with the greyhounds was non-profit. Their care was expensive, and he wondered why she did it.

He didn't see a computer or a television. Not much furniture either. What he did see were tons of books lining the walls: British classics, romance novels, medical and psychological thrillers, and suspense were just some of the genres he could make out.

"Do a little reading, do you?"

Brook smiled. "I should probably get one of those Kindle things, but I like to hold a book in my hands. Do you know anybody in need of books?

I'm ready to give away the ones lining the walls. I usually give to the nursing home in town, the one on State Street, but they told me they don't need any more."

The woman was a philanthropist.

"I can take a box for my clinic."

"That's a great idea."

He could tell by the inflection of her voice she truly liked the idea.

He checked out the rest of the room while she worked in the kitchen. Her front door was subpar. There was a chain and a lock on the knob, but no deadbolt. Daylight seeped through a huge gap between door and jamb. She needed help. She needed money. So what was she doing about getting both? He didn't want to insult her, so he didn't see how he could ask her about her financial situation. "Did you live in this house with your folks?"

She smiled as she set down Eagle's dinner. "No, we had a place over in Stoneleigh."

He knew the neighborhood. The houses were upper middle class, mostly lawyers and doctors. He guessed after her parents' death, there was no money left. No, Brook's place wasn't much to look at, but she had it disinfected to the point that it smelled like a pine forest. Various potted plants, ivy's of some type or another, were peppered around the kitchen and living room. Framed magnolia leaves hung on the wall. He suspected they were there just so she could have wall art.

He watched her prepare dinner from his vantage point in the living room. She wasn't aware he was following her every move. She wore cutoff shorts and a white tank top—he'd yet to see her in anything else. She was barefoot, having slid out of her slip-ons at the back door. She was fresh-faced—didn't she wear make-up? But why would she? She didn't need all that fake shit; she was naturally beautiful. And God, he was mooning over her like a teenager. But the realization wasn't enough to make him stop. He focused on her hair that flowed in a thick curtain to the middle of her back. She'd worn it loose yesterday too, and the thick ropes had figured prominently in a few of his more vivid daydreams that day.

Once Eagle had finished his dinner, he sat licking his face. Brook knelt over him and squeezed his narrow head to her breast and kissed him.

"You were hungry, weren't you?" For the second time in the matter of a few minutes, Cory wished he were the damn dog.

Cory turned away and took a closer look at the daybed in the living room. With two pillows at what would be the head and a water glass, alarm clock, and hand lotion on a table beside it, her living room was undoubtedly used as a bedroom.

Curious to see more of the house, he said, "I need to borrow your restroom."

Brook lifted her head. "Sure, it's just through there." With a pointed finger, she indicated the hallway.

Cory'd figured the bathroom was this way, but he couldn't just go ambling about her home without good reason. He could hear her talking to Teddy in her mothering voice as he rounded the corner. There were two doors to choose from. He opened the door nearest him. It was just as he'd suspected. What should be her bedroom was full of dog-training equipment and supplies. He closed the door and proceeded to the bathroom.

The bathroom was also in need of repairs. For starters the sink had separate hot and cold water taps. One could work with that, but it was the wrench hooked behind the faucets that worried him. The hot water dripped. The toilet was already running, and he hadn't used it. He took the lid off of the tank to inspect the internal parts. The float ball mechanism was corroded and in need of replacement. Cory placed the lid back on the tank and turned to sit on the closed toilet seat. While he didn't want to get involved romantically, he thought it might be beneficial to offer her a collaboration of sorts—strictly business of course. Someone needed to help this girl. And that someone should be him.

The spaghetti she made was nourishing and tasteful. To accompany the entrée she'd made garlic toast out of standard issue white sandwich bread, and even it was delicious. Cory was anything but fussy. He actually preferred the classics to all that fancy shit anyway.

She'd offered him a beer and served it to him in the bottle, the same way she took hers.

The woman intrigued him, a thought both exciting and frightening.

After dinner he retrieved the puppy food from his SUV. He brought it to the kitchen. He'd started opening cupboard doors in search of a container when Brook handed him a red plastic bowl. She filled another with water and set it in front of Teddy. He took two small laps. Cory prepared the mushy puppy food and placed it next to the water bowl and everyone watched, including Eagle, as Teddy slowly consumed his dinner.

Brook went to sit on the make-do couch, and Cory followed her. They sat there, the four of them playing with the squeaky toy he'd brought from his clinic. Eagle was more interested in it than Teddy was. The puppy was content chewing the laces of Cory's shoes. He picked him up by the scruff of the neck and said, "You can't be chewing stuff like that, or you'll wear out your welcome quickly."

A deep throaty giggle escaped Brook's mouth, and Cory found himself growing hard. God, he wanted to taste her again. But he couldn't. One night of sex was a fling, a good time, a one-night stand. Two nights, especially two in a row, was the start of a commitment. Unless she knew going in where he stood, he wouldn't take advantage. He cleared his throat. Did it a second time when he couldn't figure out what to say.

"Brook."

She turned half-lidded, desire-filled eyes on him. Her tongue came out and moistened her thick bottom lip. "Yeah?" Her voice was like lava, hot and melted.

Their lips crashed together. They nipped and pulled at each other with lips and teeth and tongue. She tugged at his tie and slid it free of his collar. He lifted her shirt over her head. She straddled him and set about unbuttoning his shirt. Once she had the buttons undone, she aggressively yanked it from his body. He needed to put a stop to their actions, but his hands wouldn't listen to his brain. He wanted her naked. He wanted to see her and taste her and plunge deep inside her. He reached out and cupped her breasts through her bra. She was running her hands across his chest, flicking at his nipples and tugging at his chest hair.

His mouth twitched, but no words came out. He pulled the cups of her bra down and stared at her breasts. Oh God, he wanted . . .

He swallowed painfully. "Stop. We have to stop."

Brook froze. Her brow rose as she regarded him curiously.

"I want you more than my next breath, but I can't be what you want. I don't do relationships, marriage, babies. None of that will ever exist for us." It would never exist for him.

Her head titled to the right. "How do you know I want that?"

"Isn't that what every woman wants?"

"Maybe. But someone once told me to shut off my mind and let my desire guide me."

"That person sounds like an idiot." He closed his eyes and shook his head at how stupid he'd been.

"You don't think a woman can enjoy sex just as a man does?"

"What exactly are you saying? English please."

"I'm saying I don't expect anything from you. No commitments, no preconceived obligations, no going steady, no wining and dining. I get it." She shrugged one shoulder. "I enjoyed the sex. I'm not in the habit of sleeping around, but I'd like to have more sex with you." She grinned at him. "It was fun." She pulled at one of his nipples and asked, "Wouldn't you like to play some more?"

She sucked his nipple and grabbed his crotch, then abruptly stood and shimmied out of her shorts. Either she wasn't wearing panties or she'd pulled those down with the shorts as she stood before him completely nude and glowing with desire. She was a goddess. He lifted himself up and slid out of his trousers and underwear. She climbed atop him and swept her sopping-wet cleft across his aroused cock. *Jesus.* He felt the jolt to his toes.

Wrapping her hands around his girth, Brook rose up on her knees and guided him into position. But she didn't move. He closed his eyes, couldn't hold back a groan. When she laughed softly, he looked into her eyes. Keeping her eyes on his, she slowly lowered herself until all of him was deep inside her. She set the pace and rode his cock until she was tensing and ready to go over the edge. Her voice raw, she asked, "Are you going to come? I want you to climax with me."

Cory grasped her hips to get the intensity necessary to bring him to his peak. His balls tightened, and his eyes closed with his impending release.

Brook tapped his cheek. "Hey, look at me."

It was hard for him to keep his eyes open while he ejaculated, but he was glad he did because he was rewarded. Brook was at the height of her beauty when she was aroused. To watch her spasm on top of him was the most gorgeous and sensual thing he'd ever seen. Her body flushed and simmered with electric current, and her eyes shimmered with flecks of gold.

Once they climaxed, Brook placed her arms around his neck and kissed him chastely on the mouth. She presented him with a satisfied smile and relaxed her weight against him. He sensed something behind her and tilted his head. He whispered, "Your greyhound is sitting directly behind you."

With her forehead resting on Cory's she whispered, "He can get kind of protective of me."

"He's glaring."

Her smile grew. Had he ever seen a more alluring smile? She turned in his lap to look at Eagle. "It's okay, Eagle, Cory's a nice man. He makes wonderful love to me."

Shit! Why did she have to go and ruin it with the L-word? They weren't making love. He'd thought he'd made that clear.

Damn. Damn. Damn. He threw his head back.

So now would be a good time to talk about contraceptives; that would put a damper on their "love." He cleared his throat. "Hey, uh, we haven't been using protection, and I always use protection. I don't know why I haven't been with you, but it's an issue for several reasons."

"It's okay, I'm on the pill."

She sat across his lap and trailed her fingers down his chest. He wished she'd stop that as it was distracting him. So she was on the pill. That seemed peculiar if she wasn't having sex regularly.

A loud crash rang through the room, disturbing their post-coital ease. Brook jumped up on a scream and grabbed an old warn afghan to cover her nakedness. The door had blown open. Cory reached for a pillow and held it over his penis as he walked across the room. He peeked out onto the porch, but no one was around. He pulled the door closed, opened it, and closed it again. The problem was that the latch wasn't lined up with the strike plate. He shifted a short bookcase into place against the door, to keep it shut, until he could dress and assess it further.

Brook had dressed and was staring at him with large eyes. "Since the last hurricane, things haven't worked quite right."

Cory nodded as he pulled on his pants, guessing she'd had trouble for a lot longer than a season. "Are you aware that Logan is looking for additional help during the week?"

Her forehead furrowed. "He mentioned something about that."

"Aren't you interested in extra work?"

She smiled innocently. "No, I'm good."

"You're good?"

Her smile faded. "Why don't you just tell me what you're getting at?"

He scratched the back of his head as he weighed the pros and cons of involving himself. Fuck it. "Your house needs major repairs, yet you spend most of your work week training dogs for free. It's a bit unambitious. You should work for Logan." Her mouth twisted to one side, and her brows slanted inward. He imagined it was her angry face, but he didn't feel too threatened.

"I don't remember asking you for financial advice. And I certainly don't need a life coach."

He really loathed having a serious conversation with a woman. They never reacted in a way that was reasonable. "What's with the attitude? I'm trying to help you here. I wasn't aware you knew of the available work." Cory crossed his arms. "Why don't you want to work the additional hours?"

"Usually I have three to four greyhounds at a time. I can't leave them alone for that long."

Cory nodded. He understood that. "How do you plan on tending to the repairs?" He looked around, his eyes landing on a large crack in the living room wall.

She chewed her bottom lip. "Look, more money would be nice, but it's not necessary. I manage. I've been in positions where I've had more, but I wasn't happy." Her eyes turned down, and her features looked haunted. "This life makes the most sense. I've never been more content." Her gaze followed his to the door, and she pressed her hands to her hips. "The door will hold for now."

"Do you even want to know what can be living in that crack in the wall? And the danger there," he pointed to the crack before he pointed to the door, "pales in comparison to what could happen with the door. Someone could easily get in here and hurt you. This is serious, not something to dismiss casually."

She gasped. "How easy for you to stand there and judge me. Just remember I didn't ask you to come over here." Her eyes narrowed into snakelike slits as she glared at him. "Some people need money to feel content—that doesn't work for me. And just because I don't have a private practice and a fancy degree doesn't mean I'm not ambitious."

Cory exhaled loudly through clenched teeth. "Fuck it." The house could fall down around her and all her karma bullshit. He wasn't going to press her. If she didn't want to take care of herself, there was nothing he could do to help her. He needed some space anyway. It was past time he left.

"For the record, I wasn't judging you. I was trying to help you. Thanks for the dinner." He looked to the door. "I'll go out the back."

CHAPTER 4

Corrigan St. Martin was an ass. Brook just wished he didn't have such a sweet one. Four days ago he'd walked out her back door and she'd not been able to get him out of her mind since.

When Brook stomped inside, The Good Doctor was hoppin' with a bachelorette party in progress. Logan had refused to come out from behind the counter as he stewed about a brewery hosting a bachelorette party. He was talking to himself, asking where the hell the bachelors were.

An hour later, washing and drying pint glasses wasn't enough to occupy her mind, and Brook found herself thinking of nothing but Cory. She wished he hadn't mentioned anything about the door; now she'd be leery in her own home. Imagining what she would do during a home invasion had chills crawling up her spine. What could she do? She had no means of protection. Could she afford a new door? Probably not. She had only three hundred dollars left to get her through the month.

She was in a real funk about how they'd left things. Although he was an ass, she felt she'd been harsh. He'd said he was trying to help her.

Brook had been kept busy keeping the bachelorette party in beer and peanuts, but the women were of the diva variety and not easily satisfied. The ringleader approached Brook at the bar.

"Hey, we're about to open the gifts, and I've misplaced my notepad and pen. Do you have something I can use?"

Brook dried her wet hands and pulled a couple of sheets of paper from the printer, grabbed the only writing implement she could find—a carpenter's pencil. She handed the stuff to the diva sporting a banner across her body that read *Maid of Honor*.

She reached out and took Brook's offering. "Gross, this paper is wet. Get me a pad." She slammed the paper down on the bar and scrunched up her nose at the same time. "And I need a nice gel pen, preferably blue or red—anything but black—and no pencils."

Brook stared at the woman with disbelieving eyes. They had none of those things at the bar. Brook shrugged. "There's a drugstore across the street." The maid of honor harrumphed and walked off, leaving the paper and pencil behind.

Once the gift and game portion of the festivities had been completed, the girls began to drink in earnest. Brook guessed that most of them—including the two singing very much off key—must be intoxicated considering the amount of beer they'd been ingesting. She offered them hot wings, fries, and peanuts, but they refused all food and demanded more beer. They'd become a tad belligerent for Brook's liking and had taken to calling her Beer Wench.

At eight thirty or so, Brook looked up from drafting a pitcher and into the exotic blue pools of Cory's eyes. His lips were tightly pursed until he exhaled and said, "Hey." He combed his hands through his wet hair, drawing Brook's eyes to his bulky triceps and a hint of his silky underarm hair. His T-shirt was damp and clung provocatively to his upper body. It must have been raining outside, and Brook couldn't have been more thankful. Cory looked good wet. She was completely mesmerized as she drank him in. She couldn't even speak. Only the most primitive responses were possible—breathing, pumping blood, consciousness.

Bony, pale fingers slid over his shoulder, drawing Brook out of her trance.

"Corrigan, mmm, I've missed you. Come over and have a beer with me." The maid of honor scraped her thick sculpted nails—red, of course—across Cory's wet chest. He grabbed her hand and moved it from his body. She shot a narrow-eyed look at Brook before smiling provocatively at Cory and asking, "How about a repeat of last Friday night?"

Cory's eyes caught Brook's gaze. He flexed his neck to the right. Then, still holding Brook's gaze, he said, "Julia, go scratch your claws somewhere else."

Today was Friday so that meant there had been three days between Julia and Cory when she'd been with him. Why did that bother her? He'd had Mrs. Simms the same day they'd also had sex, but the thought of him with Julia made her nauseated. She was about to walk toward the kitchen when she felt a jolt of electricity on her skin.

He reached out a hand, latched on to Brook's wrist, and pulled her out from behind the counter. "Please come with me. I need to speak with you." He never let go as he led her from the bar all the way to Logan's office. Fading in the distance, she heard the exasperated pants emanating from Julia.

He closed the office door and massaged his right temple with his fingers. "Look, Brook, I was not judging you or your lifestyle. I apologize if

I came across that way." He dug into the pocket of his jeans and pulled out a *stay and play* keychain from one of the local casinos. Attached was a copper key. "Here."

Brook held the key in front of her face. Wrinkling her nose, she asked, "What's this?"

"It's the key to your new front door."

Oh God. She'd been worried about her door situation since he'd brought it to her attention. Brook wasn't prone to crying, but her eyes blurred. She looked down to hide the tears from Cory. He put a finger under her chin and slowly tilted her face to meet his. Brook whispered, "Thank you. I don't know if you could ever understand what this means to me. No one has ever helped me like this before. Just help with no expectations. Thank you, Cory."

A few tears spilled over and down her cheeks. He wiped them away with the pads of his thumbs. "You're welcome."

The door to the office opened and in walked Logan in full-on rant mode. "There you are. It's megalomania out there. Crazy bleach-blond bachelorettes—too much peroxide has damaged their brain cells." He looked from Cory to Brook. "Something going on between you two?"

Cory offered a sly smile. "We're friends."

Logan frowned, and then he drew Brook away from Cory.

"No, no, no. I like this one, Cory, and don't intend to lose her to one of your boneheaded moves. It ain't gonna happen."

Brook ducked her head, trying to hide her smile. "I was just leaving," she said.

Logan helped her through the door, not allowing her a chance to say goodbye to Cory.

As she left, she heard them whispering. Their voices got louder the farther she moved away until she heard Cory say, "Fuck off."

Brook returned to her duties, hoping that she hadn't caused trouble between the brothers. She liked Logan, respected him even. But she couldn't help her attraction to Cory. She knew it wouldn't go anywhere—the guy hated kids and didn't want marriage, things she knew she wanted one day, but why couldn't they enjoy one another while the attraction lasted?

Brook was behind the bar washing and drying pint glasses when sinewy arms wrapped around her from behind and a pair of hands covered her eyes.

"Hey!" she yelled.

She whirled and found Parker Avants, wearing his sexy smolder, standing behind her. Parker's family owned an oyster harvesting business, and they provided oysters for the bar and brewery. His timing was great because they'd already run out of oysters for the evening.

"Hey, girl."

He leaned in to hug her, rubbing his hand across her lower back. His rich cologne made her think of passion-fueled nights. Too bad that when she pictured a man sharing those nights it wasn't Parker's face she saw.

They'd been friends since she'd started working at the brewery. Parker wanted to be more, but Brook wasn't feeling it. She thought of Cory and wondered what the difference was. They were both sexy and brooding, but Cory had an *I couldn't give a shit* attitude, and he was so arrogantly confident that picking at him was fun. He took himself way too seriously, living by some code he'd devised. Story all over town was he wouldn't date someone more than once. She'd wanted to splinter that ruse and show him he wasn't impervious to cracks within his foundation. God, when they were together it was much more than a crack, it was an explosion. And she knew he felt it too. She planned to show him she was good for more than just a few nights.

Parker's muscles had muscles and his sexy jaw line was usually covered with a few days of stubble, but Parker was just Parker. No layers. When she kissed him, it didn't jump-start her motor. When she'd kissed Cory, she could have benefited from a fire extinguisher.

Today Parker wore a tight V-neck shirt with designer jeans snug in all the right places and a belt with small spikes. He'd been in the Marines and still wore a chain of dog tags around his neck.

"Can I get you a pint?" she offered.

"Thought you'd never ask." He leaned next to her against the counter.

Brook handed him the beer. "You still available to help me pick up the animals next week?"

"Yeah, I told Dad I'd need to borrow the cargo van. I thought I'd come a bit early and take you to breakfast."

"Sounds great, I love breakfast."

"I know." Parker winked, his cheekbones highlighted by the overhead light.

They'd been out as friends so many times, she'd lost count. He'd always been gentle with her, even when she stopped him as they were rounding second base and she could feel his stiffness through his jeans. She wished she was as attracted to him as she was to Cory. Parker had the large family she'd always dreamed of belonging to. He would do anything for her and had. He was always considering what she liked and disliked. Whenever she asked him what he liked to do, he'd just shrug and say he liked being next to her. He was so nice she felt guilty at thinking him a huge bore.

The energy near the bar suddenly shifted, and Brook knew what she'd see before she turned. Cory stood directly behind her. His eyes were narrow and his head was tilted back, accentuating his chest.

"Who the hell's this guy?" He sipped his beer, never taking his eyes from her.

"Parker, meet Cory, Logan's brother. He's the new vet in town." Parker extended his hand. "Parker's family harvests those oysters you like so much."

Cory's brow rose, and his lips quirked as he extended his hand. "Is that so?"

His eyes bored into Parker as they shook hands, Cory holding on for longer than was customary. When Cory finally released him, Brook saw Parker flex the tendons in his hand. Stupid man. Evidently, he was not as unaffected by her as he put on. If so, he wouldn't be marking his territory like one of his animals.

Parker leaned in and hugged her as he said, "I gotta go, but I'll call you." He kissed her cheek and turned to Cory. "Nice meeting you."

If looks could kill, well, she'd be in trouble. Cory stabbed her with his gaze as he mumbled and huffed under his breath.

"What's that?"

"I said, what kind of name is Parker?"

"What's wrong with it?" If she didn't know any better, she'd say he was bothered by her closeness to Parker. But she knew such a thing to be ridiculous.

"It's weak." He leaned so close to her that their arms touched. Their connection sizzled.

Brook shrugged. "I like it."

He nodded. "So you and Parker, then?"

"Me and Parker?" If he wanted information, he would need to ask her outright for it. She had no intention of making any pursuit too easy for the man.

"Hey, beer wench! Get your ass over here." The scratchy shrill voice invaded their intimate conversation. Maybe a couple of minutes with the divas would give her the chance to think of new ways to tease Cory. He really needed someone to help him loosen up.

Brook threw a towel on the counter. "Excuse me, but duty calls." She grabbed two pitchers with the ladies' preferred elixir, the Penis brew.

Logan had named his brews after various organs and systems of the body. Spleen and Kidney had won awards. There were also Pancreas, Liver, Colon, and Uterus brews. As crazy as the names were, they were devised in honor of his years studying to be a doctor. He'd actually completed his pediatric residency. But he'd left medicine behind to follow his gut, which meant becoming a brewmaster. Brook understood and respected that move. He'd told her he couldn't stand the thought of someone suing him because they thought he'd put their child at risk. He'd also mentioned something about insurance companies and the game of Russian roulette they played, but she hadn't understood what he meant. He was the smartest person she'd ever met, but she sensed he was dealing with something, some overwhelming issue, that she didn't know how to help him with.

When she arrived at the bridal party's table, the maid of honor, *Julia*, started pumping her for information about her relationship status with Cory. All eyes were shifting from Brook to Julia and back again. Refusing to answer, Brook dropped off the full pitchers and reclaimed the empty ones. She returned to the sink area with Julia clacking at her heels. Brook wondered how bad the bride had to be to have deserved such a woman as her best friend.

As Brook rinsed the beer pitchers, Julia said, "Corrigan St. Martin likes to have sex with lots of women. Lots! And he doesn't serial date either. Once he has you, he's moving on. Case in point, we fucked just last week."

Brook kept her eyes focused on the task of rinsing and drying the pitchers. "I'll keep that in mind." She knew Cory did all of those things, she just didn't know why he did them. She couldn't imagine him screwing this wretched woman. Didn't most guys have a type? If Cory liked this Julia, then she couldn't see how he could have been attracted to her since they were complete opposites in looks and personality.

"He doesn't believe in marriage or conventional dating. My advice to you would be to move on and let a real woman satisfy him."

Brook turned to the obviously surgically enhanced woman and eyed her up and down. Her boobs were too high and too round to be real, her lips were injected with collagen, her nails were gelatin, her skin was overly tanned, and her hair was streaked with bleach.

"A real woman, like you? Can you even consider yourself real?"

Julia's eyes narrowed as she shot daggers at Brook and an evil smirk spread across her face. "I've never had any complaints. Least of all from Corrigan. It could be why he keeps coming back for more." Julia begin to chew lightly at the nail of her index finger.

"Thank you for the advice." Brook knew she must be lying.

"You'd do well to heed it unless you want to pick up the pieces of your broken heart from the dirt. Corrigan doesn't believe in marriage, did you hear me say that earlier? So that's not an option if it's what you're after." She surveyed Brook from head to toe. "You're a little girl, but Corrigan is a man, with a man's needs. Needs you could never satisfy like I can."

Cory stepped behind Julia. He winced and looked to Brook. "Julia, don't you think you've had enough? Why don't you go home and sleep it off."

Julia pivoted to Cory, nearly falling as she did so, and circled her index finger around on his chest. "I was just telling this little whippet of a thing the kind of woman you desire."

"That's interesting considering I just found out myself. Until recently I'd no idea I preferred whippets. I also discovered I'm very fond of freckles and fresh, clean skin, a natural woman with no enhancements or fillers."

His eyes bore into her as he spoke the words she longed to hear. "They say natural foods are good for one's diet. It turns out natural is also good for desire. Now get the hell away from her before I slap you sober. You always were a sloppy drunk."

As Julia sashayed away, she shot back, "You would know."

Brook's mind buzzed at the words Cory spoke. And her heart started jumping as well. Did he just state his type out loud? Describing her?

She quickly brought her thoughts into line—he was probably just blowing off Julia. That had to be it.

She studied him. Yeah, just as gorgeous as ever. But he didn't look like a guy who'd just declared himself.

Brook picked up a rag and started drying the area she'd drenched in water.

She knew her thoughts had been mistaken. Cory St. Martin wouldn't brag on her, declaring his interest to the world.

He rubbed his fingers on the back of his head as he looked down. "I'm sorry about her. She's always been a crazy bitch." He rubbed his head again. "The truth of it is"—his gaze roamed slowly up her body until he met her unbelieving stare—"you satisfy me more than any other woman ever has, and I need more of you."

CHAPTER 5

Cory sat on Brook's daybed, reading a psychological thriller. He and Brook had come to an agreement—getting together for sex whenever the mood struck. And the mood had struck every day—sometimes two and three times a day—for the past several days. They'd had sex at her house, in his office, at the stables out at his house. He couldn't get enough. And she seemed just as hooked. But he'd made it clear it was sex and sex only. Well, that and seeing that a few repairs were done on her house. Nothing big, just some basics. There was no reason for her to make do with problems when he could so easily replace a faucet and buy parts for her toilet.

He was at a hair-raising scene when a car door slammed out in the street. He heard the snick of a key in lock, and the door opened to reveal Brook on the threshold, admiring the new red front door. There had been something new for her to admire everyday. Yesterday he'd had all the screens replaced, the day before that he'd had a new set of steps delivered for the back entrance.

Cory watched as she slid her palm across the glossy paint and grasped the nickel-finished handset. She pushed it closed and leveled her green eyes on him. Her gaze was lush, like a tropical forest canopy capable of devouring him. As she walked toward him, she shimmied out of her skirt and pulled her shirt over her head. She eased between his legs and bent to kiss him lightly on the mouth as her hands palmed his head.

No words needed to be exchanged. Cory pulled the cups of her bra down and was rewarded with the sight of her nipples growing hard and dark. He grasped the mounds in his hands and sucked them into his mouth, one after the other, licking and tasting and suckling. Brook pressed closer, her breath catching, and he drew from her breast even harder. He loved the taste of her tits, her skin. Loved making her go wild.

He licked a trail from her chest to her navel and while he played with her, he slid her panties down and off. When he was satisfied, he leaned back and stared at her clad in only cowboy boots. Now that was pretty. And damned arousing.

Still fully clothed, he stood and pulled her to a recliner. With one hand between her shoulder blades and one at her neck, he eased her down and positioned her with her stomach across the arm of the chair. Using his foot, he spread her legs wide and pushed her deeper into the chair, lifting her ass until the lips of her cunt spread and revealed her bubble-gum-pink channel.

Cory groaned. Using his index and middle fingers, he massaged her lips, spreading around her wetness. When Brook's breathing changed, he walked around to stand in front of the chair, where her head rested. Her eyes followed him. He removed his shirt and unbuttoned his fly slowly, watching Brook's eyes track his hands, and slid his pants down, pulling them from his body. Looping his thumbs into the waistband of his boxers, he pushed them down and gripped his raging hard-on.

Cory stood naked in front of Brook with a painfully engorged cock, stroking himself from root to tip. Her groan was low and hoarse as she watched him masturbate. His strokes started slow and steady, but turned violent. When he was ready to come, he pressed his cock to her lips. "Open," he said. She did, and he spewed his seed into her mouth. She greedily swallowed him down. He pulled free of her mouth, but stepped closer to her. He stroked her cheek as he worked to catch his breath. But she made that hard for him by nuzzling his cock and his thighs, rubbing against him. Licking wherever she could reach.

"Damn, why do I want you so much?"

She had him twisted up inside, but he still couldn't get enough. And he felt damned good when he was with her. It wasn't right that a woman should make him feel so good.

He moved around the chair to stand between her spread legs.

"Please, Cory. Don't make me wait."

He reached for her ass with both hands, alternately rubbing and kneading. She squirmed as he did, her mouth releasing sounds that drove him crazy. Sounds that made him hard again. He smacked her on the right globe of her ass. She let out a squeal of surprise. He cupped the spot, trapping the heat under his hand. She moaned. He repeated the smack to her left cheek and then thrust deep into her from behind. From this position his cock could press deep, and he sank to the root, causing Brook to gasp on a choked cry. He gave her a few seconds before he pulled slowly out and then he drove in again, starting a frenetic pace.

Cory spread his legs and used her hips to rock her back and forth on his shaft, but he wanted her to feel more.

"Touch yourself, baby. Rub your clit."

She shifted and slid one hand between her legs. The other she used as leverage against the chair.

The wet slaps against her sex and her own fingers brought her quickly to ecstasy; Cory felt moisture flood her, rush over his cock, and used it to increase his speed. She cried out his name and squeezed around him, gripping and sucking him deeper. God, he was going to die, it felt so good. "Ah, fuck." He stilled her hips and shot thick ropes of cum deep inside her again and again, until the last tremble left his body.

He knew he should help her up, rub the kinks out of her back and legs, but he couldn't move. He simply could not pull away.

After a few moments, with both of them breathing heavily, Brook put her hands under her and pushed. He got the message and lifted away, helping her upright as he did so. She steadied herself against the chair and he ran his hands over her hips and thighs, once again kneading her flesh. But this time he sought to comfort rather than arouse. He pressed close when she stretched, and when she dropped her hands over his back and pulled his head close to hers, he went willingly. They stood unmoving until their hearts finally settled.

And then Cory carried a laughing Brook over to the daybed, lowered himself into it without dropping her, and then held on to her, eyes closed, heart content. This was a first for Cory, snuggling after sex. He didn't understand it, but he knew he needed to be near her, as close as he could get. If his dick wouldn't scream at him for doing it, he'd cram himself inside her even as they simply sat quietly.

"Cory?"

"Yeah, babe."

"You know I don't care about Julia or any other woman you've had, but I do care about you, so I'd like you to explain something to me."

She never demanded anything of him and gave him so much, so he figured she deserved an answer or two. "Sure. What is it?"

"What did she mean when she said you don't *believe* in marriage?"

Shit, she certainly went for the big one with that question. He'd heard that women got introspective after sex but since he usually took off before they could ask him questions, he hadn't been prepared for what Brook might say.

Still, he'd told her to ask.

He'd never explained to anyone where his notions about marriage came from. To do so would be like exposing himself, exposing the inner man. But he knew that Brook wouldn't use the information to manipulate him. He'd watched her, listened to her, with others. She didn't use their frailties to hurt them. He dropped his head to her shoulder and sighed. He'd never thought that about a woman before Brook, that he could trust her. He'd thought women were all out to get what they could, any way they could.

He shifted a bit and reached one arm around Brook so he could reach her breast. He stroked absently, wanting, needing, that connection. She wrapped one leg around his and curved her fingers over his other hand and pressed it to her belly. He wanted to laugh—was she protecting him or making sure he didn't pull away?

He swallowed down the lump in his throat.

"When I was twelve, my father took all the kids to a ballgame. All except me. I couldn't go because I had strep throat. I'd just woken from a fever induced nap when I walked into my parents' bedroom and saw my mother packing up her things. She hadn't mentioned she was going anywhere, but she had all her cases out and was loading them with clothes and personal items—photographs, jewelry, collectable bottles, and other items. When I asked her where she was going, she told me to go back to bed. Something . . . something wasn't right. When I asked what was going on, she again told me to go to my room. Then she ignored me.

"I walked to the hallway but that's as far as I got. I slumped against the wall and watched her. She had the driver collect her bags and load them into the car. When she came out of her bedroom, I asked her again what was going on. She said, 'Grow up, boy, what does it look like? I'm leaving.' I remember asking her if she were mad at me. She told me not to be ridiculous and that it had everything to do with my father. At that time I couldn't understand why she couldn't just overlook whatever he'd done and work it out, just like she and Dad had always told us to do. I guess I still don't understand that. There are seven of us, and Clara was barely walking and talking back then. You'd think that seven children, one of them a toddler, would be a reason to stay and attempt to work things out. Plus Dad was never around, so what was to become of us?" He laughed, though no one would mistake it for a cheerful sound. "I just couldn't believe she'd leave like that."

Cory's chest began to tighten, as it did whenever he gave more than a passing thought to those days. He took deep cleansing breaths, and Brook turned in his arms to face him. She grasped his hands firmly in hers.

"Cory, it's okay. You d—"

"When she started down the staircase, I wrapped my fingers around her leg and begged her not to go. I cried and carried on, believing that if she really knew how much I wanted her to stay, she would. I howled like I'd never cried before, but it didn't change anything. She . . . she called the stable manager to pull me off and hold me away from her as she left. She let someone—made someone—keep me away from her. I screamed at her not to go. Bill released me once we heard her car start up, and I ran after the car as it drove down the long and winding drive. I never caught her."

Unable to take Brook's compassion any longer, he rearranged them until he was once again behind her, his arms wrapped around her.

"She was gone. And I was devastated. She didn't come around much after that. She has started to these past few years, but I don't know why. It can't be for any good reason. The years that counted the most have already passed. She should never have come back."

Brook didn't say anything. She just lightly stroked his forearm with her fingertips. Her breath was slow and her heartbeat even, exposing his erraticism even more. Her calm confidence helped center and relax him.

"I can understand your skepticism regarding marriage. I can't understand what that must have been like, to have a parent abandon you, but surely you know that not all marriages are like your parents' marriage."

"My skepticism? Call it what it is—cynicism. That contract they give you, you know the one that you sign? It means nothing to anyone. My brother wasn't married six months when he walked in on his wife going at it full throttle in *their* bed with another man. I'm not the only cynic in the family."

Brook once again turned herself around until they were face to face. She used her thumb and index finger to push aside the hair hanging in his eyes. Then she kissed his brow.

"No, you aren't the only skeptic. Do you plan to have a family?"

"You mean like kids?"

"Yeah, kids."

"Well, no. I'm not going to have a bastard child."

"So what's your grand plan?"

"My only plan is to remain a free man. I don't want to lead you on. No marriage. No kids. No family."

***

Things were not good. For starters, Brook was pretty sure she was falling hard for Cory. But she was pretty sure that he wasn't falling for her.

He liked her, yes. Liked having sex with her, double yes. But he was adamant about not pursuing a future with her. She knew it wasn't her—he'd set his attitude about marriage long before they met. But what woman didn't want to be the one to break through to her man's heart? That didn't look likely with Cory.

And then there was the kid issue. When she'd asked him about kids last night, she knew what he would say. Cory didn't want a wife and he would never father children and then abandon them after what he went through, so that meant no children. Brook didn't know how she felt about having children in the near future but when she envisioned herself as an old woman, her children and their children always surrounded her. She knew she wanted kids eventually. She wanted as many as she could have so that she would finally get her large, loving family.

Anything long term looked to be out of the question for them. So did that mean she should break it off, start looking for someone else?

But how did you break off a relationship when the ties were still so strong?

A knock at her door pulled her from her thoughts. Parker, looking like sex on a stick, was ready to take her to breakfast. She wished she was attracted to him. Things would have been so much easier. He played no games, had no hidden agenda.

"I like your new door."

"Thanks." She smiled at him, and he kissed her cheek, as he always did.

"Waffle House?"

"Perfect." He even knew her tastes.

He held the door to the van open for her and made sure she was securely inside before he closed it. A woman smarter than Brook needed to snatch him up soon.

They had a full morning and by noon had unloaded the animals at the stables on the St. Martin estate.

"This is a nice place." Parker looked out across the vast expanse of land.

Brook was busy pulling supplies out of the van. "Isn't it? Randy is buried down by the pecan grove."

Parker leaned in to the van next to Brook and studied her. She read the curiosity in his metal-gray eyes.

"What?" she asked.

"So you really like this guy."

Was he telling her? Because she sure didn't hear a question in his words.

He was watching her every move, trying to read her. She knew how he felt about her and she felt bad, but thought it best to tell him the truth.

"He's a good guy. He can seem a bit prickly at times, but he really is genuinely nice."

Parker crossed his arms. "And so . . . ?"

"And so . . . Yes, I like him."

Parker's jaw tensed, and he closed his eyes. Brook's stomach tightened as she watched him.

"It was never going to be me, was it then?" He lowered his gaze to her hands, clasped them in his. "I knew that. I lost count of the number of times you said I was such a great friend."

He placed his palm on her cheek and his eyes darkened with a need she would never be able to answer.

"What the fuck's going on here?" A low, hoarse voice shattered the tense moment. Brook was relieved and then troubled.

She gasped and whipped her head in Cory's direction. "Cory!"

His brow furrowed as he glared over the tops of his aviator shades and took in the intimacy of her position next to Parker.

Stepping away from Parker, Brook said, "We were just unloading the animals into the stables."

Cory huffed and swore violently, not quite under his breath, as he stomped into the stable yard. He rubbed the back of his head as he took in the scene. "What the hell?" He turned to Brook. "You said you were bringing the rescue dogs here."

"There are two over there." She pointed behind him and to the right.

Cory turned. "But that isn't a greyhound, it's a three-legged mutt with mange." He gestured to the corner. "And is that a pregnant goat?"

"Both the mutt and the goat had to come with me. They were due to be euthanized today."

Cory's head went back as he raised his eyes to the sky and exhaled a long breath, a very long breath, through clenched teeth. "Jesus, Brook. Are you going to rescue all the animals on death row?"

"Not all. Just the ones I can."

"You won't even make a difference. Thousands are put to death *every day* in the state of Louisiana alone."

Brook's eyes filled with tears as she bent to pick up the three-legged dog. "It makes a difference to this one."

He shook his head, but he walked to her and wrapped one arm around her. "Your heart is simply too big. Here . . . " He put the mange-infested mutt on the ground and then grasped her shoulders. "Please don't cry. We have plenty of room here. It should be fine. Just don't bring any more. The last thing I want to do is come home to a bunch of mangled and sick animals at the end of the day. I'll need to treat this dog." He carried the dog over to a corner of the stable. Brook and Parker followed. Cory was silent as he filled a bucket with water and some solution he pulled from a shelf. He pulled on a pair of gloves and dipped the squirming dog into the bucket.

She hadn't considered that he'd have to come home to do more work. But she should have. Her heart was no bigger than his.

"Brook?"

She turned to Parker.

"I've got to run a few errands. Do you want to go with me?" He shrugged. "Or I can come pick you up when I'm done."

"I'll take care of her," Cory said, not even bothering to turn.

Parker's lips tightened, and his chest expanded slightly. "Brook?"

"Yeah, I'll just get Cory to give me a ride home, but thanks for all your help today and for breakfast."

Parker hugged her and whispered, "You sure you're cool with me leaving?"

She shook him off when she felt Cory's gaze burning through them. "Yeah, it's fine. Thanks again." She waved as he walked out.

She watched a moment before she turned and stormed over to Cory. She narrowed her eyes at him. "Why do you always have to be so moody and mean?"

"He's always got his hands all over you." He rinsed the dog with water from a hose.

Brook pointed to the spot where the van had been parked. "Parker's my friend."

Cory raised his brow and tilted his head in her direction. "Seems like more than friends."

"What do you mean?"

"Did I not give you enough last night? I guess not. Considering how you're dressed, I figure you're trolling for sex."

Brook looked down at her clothes. Shorts and a tank is what she always wore to deal with the unbearable heat. "There is something seriously wrong with you." She would walk home. It didn't seem that far. She headed out to the driveway.

Cory followed. "Are you so mad because what I said is true?"

"I'm mad because I just realized what an idiot I've been to think emotion and sex could be isolated. After observing your behavior, it's clear that they can't be separated."

"My behavior?"

"Yes, yours. Or didn't you notice yourself stewing in a sea of jealousy? You have so many commitment issues that you should lock your thing up until you straighten them out, but instead you just take out your problems on innocent women."

"Women are anything but innocent. You shouldn't even use the words in the same sentence."

Brook abruptly stopped and whirled around. Her eyes wide, she asked, "What part of *I don't sleep around* did you not understand?"

Cory shrugged. "All of that terminology is relative. You weren't a virgin when I first had you, so clearly you've been sleeping with somebody. And then you're on the pill, that's convenient."

Whack! The sound hit her just before the seething pain screamed through her hand. She'd slapped his stupid face. Attraction be damned, there wasn't enough great sex in the world that would have her putting up with his bullshit.

CHAPTER 6

Cory recoiled, feeling as if a two-by-four had been rammed into his face. "Goddammit, Brook!" His hand went to his cheek. It was hot from the rush of blood where she'd slapped him.

She'd already turned and was pounding down the road. Crazy woman; where did she think she was going to go? Their land went for miles in either direction. And where the hell had she developed that right hook?

It would be dark before she even reached the main road. He went back for his SUV and caught up with her in moments.

"Get in the damn truck."

She turned her flushed, tear-stained face to him. Fuck, she was crying. His chest immediately burned. He pushed two fingers into it to relieve the pain.

"Why are you crying?"

"I'm crying because you don't know shit that you think you know. You hurt me and any other woman that comes across your path. Instead of using your fortune for good, you use it to demolish. You're like a tornado."

What the hell was she talking about? Women were all bat-shit crazy. "I'm sorry, but I don't follow." He didn't even know why he bothered asking her to explain.

She stepped up to the open passenger-side window and threw her arms in the air. "You have the face and body of a god. And you know it too. You have a great practice—people trust you with their animals because you're good and caring. And yeah, you have the family name and reputation behind you. And yet you use all sorts of defense mechanisms to hide your feelings. And don't even get me started about how you use sex. Even if love were all around, you wouldn't see it because the sex would be in the way." Rubbing her forehead, she sighed. "You have a community that supports you *in spite of* your many irresponsible sexual conquests, including those

44

with married women." She pointed a finger at him. "You better be on the lookout for a few pissed-off husbands. No matter what you think about their virility, no man wants another man's hands on his woman." She stepped back and crossed her arms. "Your family supports your every move and desire. You are blessed abundantly, but you're so jaded you can't see what you have right in front of you. Do you even know that most people would kill to have what you have?"

She ended on a deflated sigh and her body slumped forward.

Cory put the car in park and jumped out.

"Just a damned minute. You don't know what the hell you're talking about." He circled the SUV and stopped next to Brook.

"You have no right to say that." He stabbed a finger into the air near her chest. "Who are you to say that?"

Brook simply shook her head. She didn't back away and she didn't blink at his anger.

"You know it's true. Do you deny that you have so many gifts? Not all of them were handed to you—I know you worked your butt off to become a vet. I know you take care of the family property. But you *have* been blessed. You have it all." She reached out both hands and trapped one of his between them. "Or almost all."

He froze. And then he was the one pulling back, the one stepping away. She'd nailed him. It was all true—he had a lot of support but he habitually dismissed it because he didn't have the support of the one person who meant the most to him. His mother. She'd left, had turned her back, and he'd turned his back on anyone who offered him the support he'd wanted from her. He squeezed his eyes closed. If she, his own mother, hadn't considered him worthy of support, of love, he knew he had no business accepting it, searching for it, from others.

Shit. Wasn't he fucked up?

And now that his mother was trying to reinstate herself into their lives like nothing had happened, he pushed even harder against anyone who reached out to him. He didn't want to be reminded of that time, of not being enough for her. Of not being enough.

But Brook hadn't pulled back. And she had seen straight into him.

He grasped her hips and slid his hands up to her slim waist. She seemed so thin. Thinner than when they'd met. Her body went limp in his hands and her head fell back. Oh God. He opened the car door and placed her on the seat. He shook her shoulder and patted her face.

"Brook?"

Her eyes rolled under the lids before they opened as tiny green slits.

"Brook?" His voice cracked, and his heart hammered in his chest.

"Hmm." She smiled softly.

"Brook, baby, look at me."

She opened her eyes wider and slowly sat up, balancing herself with one hand on the dash. "I'm so tired."

"You passed out." He brushed the hair out of her eyes with a shaky hand.

"Will you please drive me home?"

Despite his questions, she was quiet the entire drive to her house.

He unlocked her front door with the key he'd made for himself and let them inside. Eagle and Teddy were there to greet her. She bent to pick up Teddy, but he leaped from her arms and into Cory's. She dropped onto the daybed, and Eagle hurried over and rested his head in her lap.

Cory remained by the door, unsure of what to say. She hadn't wanted to stop for food, but now he wondered if he shouldn't have overruled her. She looked pale as she rubbed Eagle's head. Maybe she was still stewing. He'd never seen her as angry as she was back at the stables.

"I'm sorry for upsetting you earlier."

She nodded before she caught his gaze. Her forehead wrinkled, "It's important for me to know that you understand, I don't sleep around."

He didn't really believe that she did. Seeing Parker's hands on her had him instinctively territorial and he'd acted like an ass. "I never believed you did."

She held her hand up indicating she had more to say. "After my parents died, I went to live with my uncle and his wife. I was nine. I'd lived in Whisky Cove my entire life. New Jersey was different. Their house was different. It seemed cold and unloving. At nine years old I realized my old life with my parents had been like a really good dream, a dream I could always go back to when things got tough and I needed to feel real comfort and sincere love. I dreamed of them every night for months."

Her voice lacked inflection and she stared, unfocused, at Eagle. "My uncle is a bastard and a drunk. I would hear him come home late at night and yell and hit his wife. I was afraid of him, so I stayed out of his way. I'd wanted to ask Shelly why she stayed with him and let him abuse her, but selfishly I thought of myself and what would become of me if she were to leave. So I thought it best not to ask."

Cory joined her on the bed. He placed his arm around her and pulled her tight to his side. He kissed her temple. "You were a child. You can't blame yourself for her poor decisions."

"When I was eighteen I witnessed the worst fight they'd had. She was bleeding. To my knowledge, that was a first. I jumped in then, but ended up taking a fist to the face. After that I knew I had to get out of there.

"The one thing that kept me sane through it all was Randy. My aunt and uncle breed and train show collies. I picked up my skills as a handler from them. I met someone—a guy. He promised to make all my dreams come true." She laughed. "I know. I was a fool to believe him. I left my uncle's home and moved in with Joey. He had a large family and they all lived together. They accepted me with unconditional love. We lived in his room. We were young. Idiots. It was a mistake but still, it was the happiest time I'd known since my parents died. I loved his family and because of that, because of them, it was easy to overlook the fact that he slept with any and everything that crossed his path."

She turned to Cory then, her smirk clearly sarcastic. "Seriously, anything. Men and women alike, or both at the same time."

"The East Coast is a strange place," Cory murmured.

Her smirk relaxed into a true smile, and Cory hugged her.

"I decided I wanted to come back to Whisky Cove and saw an ad in the Herald for a greyhound handler at the park. I took the job and bought this house. I've been happy here."

She frowned, and Cory watched her jaw tighten.

"I'm not in the habit of lying. I told you all this"—she waved a hand in front of their faces—"to show you that when I said I'd been with one man, it was the truth." She pulled out of his hold. "Parker and I have made out, but that's it."

He pulled her body back against his side and turned her face toward his with his finger. "Brook." He bent toward her and sucked her bottom lip into his mouth. When he released it, he kissed it tenderly. "I'm a dumbass. Of course you weren't lying." He shook his head. "I don't like seeing you with Parker. I especially don't like him putting his hands on you. I have no right to feel that way and didn't even know I did." God, the thought of Parker touching her, making out with her, had him seeing red. He wanted to put a hit on Parker's head. He'd have to tell her.

He dragged his hand across his lips and chin. "Until today I hadn't thought I'd ever be monogamous, but I'd like to be with you. The truth is, since that night at the deer stand, I haven't been able to even think about sex with anyone else. I don't know how you feel, but would you consider being exclusive?"

Brook smiled her ridiculously large and revealing smile at him. "Are you asking me to go steady?"

"Make sure you share the news with Parker," Cory said in response to her snarky enthusiasm.

She pressed her lips to his and placed one palm on his cheek as she kissed him tenderly. Cory's hands slid into her thick nut-brown hair, and his tongue explored her mouth. But he had one more task before they could get lost in one another. He pulled his mouth away from the sweetness of hers.

"Brook, I'm sorry I said what I did about the way you were dressed. I was lashing out after seeing you stand so close to Parker. I didn't mean to hurt you." He dropped a swift kiss to her mouth. "I rather like the way you dress. It keeps me hot and bothered."

"Apology accepted. Now kiss me."

He pushed Teddy aside—he wasn't sure how the puppy had gotten between them. And then they were kissing in earnest. The sweet moans that came from her throat were his undoing. He wanted to spend every second of the day with her. He'd attempted to distance himself these last weeks, but every time he swore to himself that the day would not end with her in his arms, he'd lost the battle. Truth told, he was tired of fighting his body, and he was tired of fighting his body. Hell, his mind too as it flashed pictures of their intimacy like a closed-loop movie. He cared for her, and the thought crossed his mind that fifty years from now he still would not have had his fill of her. That possibility scared the shit out of him. But God, she felt so right in his arms.

When he was young his parents had taken him to a rain forest conservatory. It had been filled with gorgeous, exotic butterflies. Brook's beauty and personality reminded him of a butterfly fluttering around. Positive energy poured out of her and into him. He'd been walking around with a dark cloud of moodiness hanging over his head these past few weeks. Now that he knew she was exclusively his, the melancholia immediately abated.

His hand slid under her shirt and moved across her velvet skin, reaching her breast and cupping it tenderly in his palm. As he molded its shape, his thumb and finger pinched the engorged tip. Brook broke free of his mouth and groaned out some mangled version of his name. He laughed, knowing he had her. He loved that he could turn her on, that she responded so eagerly to him. She opened her eyes and bright as sunbeams, they beckoned him like a moth to a flame.

"You're naturally beautiful but when desire courses through your veins, you are a goddess. I can't resist you." And he couldn't resist the poetic. She was like a muse, encouraging him. He removed her shirt and bra and unfolded their bodies across the bed. He grazed her nipple with his teeth. When she cried out, he soothed her sensitive skin with the flat of his tongue. As he provided the same attention to the other breast, Brook's delicate hands started to unbutton his shirt. She trembled as she always did once they started exploring each other's bodies, once they started driving one another toward climax. No woman had ever responded to him like she did, as if his every touch burned her. Her hands shook with the energy coursing through her, and he placed his over hers and said, "Together."

When his shirt was off, she wiggled a bit, indicating she wanted to shift positions, and Cory gave in to her demands. She sat atop him in just her cutoff shorts. She leaned down and slithered her tongue over the muscles of his chest. Her body sensuously moved left to right as she tasted every inch of his upper body. When she started in on his oblique muscles, he shifted, trying not to laugh. She jerked her head up and offered him a saucy smile. She quirked her brow and then laid into his side using teeth, tongue, and fingers. Cory couldn't catch his breath from laughing. His erection was harder than it had ever been and when he thrust his hips up at her, she immediately stopped playing games and rocked against his cock with her wet heat.

He unbuttoned her shorts, and she rose on her knees so he could slide her shorts and panties down her legs. When she sat back down, she threw her legs over the side of the bed and pushed her clothes free of her body. Then she undid his trousers and pulled them away from his body. When she finished, she took up her position straddling his lap.

Slick soft heat snuggled his dick. "Do you like cowgirl?" she asked, slanting her head to one side.

"I like it when you do it."

Her brow furrowed. "Do you have a favorite position?"

"I never really thought about it." It was hard for him to think coherently about anything when she was spreading her juices all over his erection.

"Hmm. A good project might be to try them all and rank them based on pros and cons." She kept gyrating over him.

He swallowed. "I like a worthy project; count me in."

Plump folds of wet hotness engulfed his cock as she lowered herself on him. He gasped at the heat. She clutched him in her tightness like dark grips the depths of the ocean floor. He knew nothing else in that moment but her hypnotic writhing and the fisting, convulsing inner walls of her sex.

On her knees astride him, she arched back and then kept going, her hands sliding to his ankles and her shoulders resting just below his knees. Jesus, she was holding him and open to him at the same time. When she didn't move, he pushed himself up and bent forward to check on her, wondering if she'd passed out again. Hell no, she was in bliss. He hovered over her body and wrapped his arms around her, just above her hips. Her back bowed and came to rest between his legs. In that position she was laid out before him like a buffet. Her tits were thrust in his face when she started to move. Her hips and thighs pumped her up and down, and he stretched forward to suck at the breasts that were begging to be tasted.

Oh God, he would never last. Not with her under him, over him, riding him. Not with her in his hands and eyes and surrounding his cock. It was too much. They were connected deep within her body, yet he felt as if she was inside him. And when the first quiver shook his sac, he knew he was about to come.

And that's when Brook breathlessly whispered his name.

In that moment he knew, it was about more than the awesome sex they shared. He knew he would still want her with as much force even if sex were not on the table. He just needed to be with her and he needed to know that she would never leave him.

CHAPTER 7

Brook was in love with Cory, that much was certain. She wanted to tell him, felt that he should know, but she didn't want to spook him. Over the last couple of weeks she'd sensed he'd changed. He was still challenging, which she loved, but there was tenderness and a reverence about him when he touched her or looked into her eyes. She hoped that was due to love.

Due to a huge Louisiana State University ball game, the brewery was hoppin'. She'd been sick to her stomach earlier and now she was exhausted, but she pressed on as the customers emptied the beer taps. When she had a dizzy spell, Logan pulled her to his office and closed the door.

He sat her in a chair and knelt in front of her as he took her pulse. "I heard you were sick earlier. How long's that been going on?"

"I don't know. I think it was some old eggs. I really need to throw that carton out."

"You've been tired too." He stood and placed his palm on her forehead. He pushed her head back and looked at her pupils.

"When was your last period?"

Her eyes went wide. "What? I'm not telling you that."

He shrugged one shoulder. "Why not? I am a doctor."

"You're not *my* doctor," she said. But she did think about his question. She scratched her head. "I don't think I had it this month."

Logan's eyes squinted to slits as he placed his elbow on his desk and watched her. "Any breast tenderness?"

"Yes!" Brook thought it was strange, but her boobs had been painfully sore. She'd written the pain off to jogging in a regular bra instead of a sport bra.

"You're pregnant."

Logan's demeanor was so matter of fact, she had to recast what he'd said.

She couldn't hold back a disbelieving laugh. "Not possible; I'm on the pill."

"It's very possible; in fact, it's true. You're pregnant. I would estimate six weeks. Although you would know better than I would."

Six weeks. That was when Randy had died. Oh God, this wasn't happening. Not when things were going so well with Cory. Tears leaked from her eyes.

Warm hands covered hers.

"Hey, I'm here. I'll help you, but you'll have to trust and talk to me. I'm assuming from your tears you are aware of Cory's thoughts about marriage and children."

She snapped her head up and stared into Logan's eyes. Her brows drew together. "Our relationship just took a turn for the better. This will throw him for a loop. No, more than that." Her hands went to her mouth as she inhaled on a gasp. "He will hate me."

"Are you aware of your options?"

"Options?"

"I'm only sharing the options with you. This doesn't mean I think you should do any particular one of them. There's a pill you can take to terminate, up to nine weeks after your last menstrual period."

She shook her head furiously, one hand on her stomach. "Never!"

"Okay, that's good. So you want this baby." Logan caressed her shoulder.

Brook suddenly thought of Cory. Would he want her to abort the child? She wouldn't do it. Now that she thought about it, this was the best thing Cory could have given her. It was a chance for her to have what she'd always wanted—a family. She would protect the child in her belly with her life. She could leave. The greyhound park in Galveston had called just last week asking if she could fill in for a few months. That would be enough time for her to safely develop the baby in her stomach.

Logan eyed her suspiciously. Then he crossed his arms. Damn, he'd always been too smart for her liking. He inhaled a deep, audible breath. "You're gonna walk."

"I have to. I don't know how much you know about your brother, but Cory's greatest fear is marriage and kids. I won't stay here and force him into something he doesn't want. Or worse, he could talk me into doing something *I* don't want. After what happened with your mother, if he were to ask me to stay, I'd never be able to leave. He'll feel obligated. But I don't want him to have regrets and think of me and a baby as an obligation. That would kill me."

"I get it, but please let me help you."

Brook didn't know how he could help, but she promised not to do anything without consulting him. And she got him to promise that he wouldn't say or do anything to tip Cory off in any way.

The next day Brook baked up a batch of blueberry muffins using the berries her neighbor had so kindly given her. She needed to see Cory one more time before she left, wanting to memorize his face, his touch, his voice. She secured the warm muffins in a basket and placed a tea towel over the top, then she rode her bike to the clinic. She walked in and saw three clients waiting, holding their pets on their laps. No one was at the counter, so Brook rounded the corner for Cory's office.

When she opened the door their eyes met and his smile engaged. He was on the phone speaking to someone about a horse that was evidently very sick. He held his arm out, inviting her to join him. When his call ended, he bent down to kiss her. "I like it when you visit me at work."

"I brought you some muffins." She held one out to him.

His blue eyes sparkled like wet ice. "Mmm, still warm." He took a bite that demolished most of the cake.

Now that she was there, she didn't know what to say. Before she could say anything, his office door crashed open, and two blond-headed boys stood in the doorway. One was dressed as a superhero, complete with cape. The other carried a plastic sword. The one in the cape took off and ran to hide under Cory's desk. The other boy ran after him, chasing him out from his hiding place. They crashed into the wall, and Cory's books and trophies fell to the floor.

"Christ! Where's your mother?"

Brook winced. She'd never heard Cory yell so loudly before. He grabbed each boy by their collars, as if he were picking up puppies, and narrowed his eyes at them. "Do you know what happens to bad little boys?" Their eyes went wide at his sinister voice. "At night when you lie down to sleep—"

"Come on, let's see if we can find your mom." Brook broke in. "She must be around here somewhere." Their mother was Cory's receptionist; no one else would allow her children to run wild in a professional setting. Yet even though they were the ones running wild, Brook was appalled at the horrible things Cory had been about to say to them. They would have nightmares for eternity.

She'd seen the glint in his eye, but she knew the boys hadn't.

Once she delivered the children to Amanda, she returned to Cory's office. She joined him as he picked up the items that littered the floor. Within moments, strong arms circled her waist.

"Thanks, Brook."

She turned around, and Cory peppered kisses along her neck. She pulled out of his hold. "You were deliberately trying to scare those children."

"Those two are Satan's spawn. I don't want to fire their mother, but I'm trying to work here. Besides, you know I can't stand kids."

Brook's head shot up, "You can't stand them?"

He exhaled noisily. "Haven't we been over this?"

"I thought you didn't want marriage and therefore wouldn't have children. I didn't know you loathed them."

"Well, I do, the monsters, so it's just as well I'll never be in a position to have them."

So . . . she'd been mistaken all along. Thank God he'd straightened her out, otherwise she might have been tempted to tell him what was going on. Knowing it was the last time she'd see him, she took her time, sharing muffins with him and then aligning all the knickknacks that had fallen from his shelves after he went to see his next patient. She did it all with a smile, not intending to give anything away, but she felt as if knives were sawing at her insides, slicing at her heart.

Less than two hours later, she had Logan drive her and Eagle to the bus station in the next town. When she exited Logan's truck and stepped into the hot sun, she felt an overwhelming heaviness settle on her. He helped her carry her stuff inside and he purchased her ticket, all the while trying to convince her to stay. She explained, again, her situation and he finally said he understood how hard it would be for her to stay. Brook hugged him hard, unleashing the emotion she hadn't been able to give to Cory.

With tears streaming down her face, she waved goodbye to Logan from her spot at the back of the bus.

Eagle looked worried, so she plopped down in the seat next to him and opened his kennel door. She reached her hand in to stroke between his ears.

"We're going to be all right, Eagle. It's just you and me now." She rubbed her belly. "And soon there will be one more."

CHAPTER 8

As Cory unlocked the red front door of Brook's home, he knew she wouldn't be there. He could feel the lack of spark and energy. He opened the door, and Teddy came running up to him. He gathered the little fellow up and found a note attached to his collar. Cory pulled the note free.

Cory,

You need Teddy and he needs you. I can't explain why, but I had to leave. It was necessary and dictated by events beyond my control. I need you to understand that I didn't want to leave. Had things been different, I would have stayed by your side forever. I never want you to regret anything that happened between us—I won't. Not ever. I'll see you in my dreams. I'll feel you inside me at night when I lie down to sleep. Having experienced it for the first time with you, I'll never forget what love feels like. What it's supposed to feel like. I hope you can find a way to be happy. You deserve so much more than what you are allowing yourself to have. You are the most generous person I've ever met. I'll cherish our time together for the rest of my life.

I love you,

Brook

Cory staggered to the recliner in the living room and dropped awkwardly into the seat. She was gone. Forever gone. The woman he loved had abandoned him. It had happened again.

He re-read the letter. Something beyond her control? What was it? Why hadn't she confided in him? He felt helpless and out of control. She was gone and she'd left him with no answers, no way to find her. He examined the room. No, she hadn't left any other message. She didn't want him to find her. He tried to imagine what could have happened, but nothing came to mind.

He wondered if something had happened at the brewery and briefly thought of checking with Logan, but then it hit him like a bullet to the chest—Parker. Brook's leaving had something to do with that son of a bitch.

Cory drove to the brewery. He needed answers, and he would kill to get them.

He stalked inside and searched the place. Problem was, he didn't know what he was searching for. Then his eyes found Parker waiting for his turn at one of the pool tables. He strode up to him, grabbed him by the neck, and yelled, "Where is she?"

Parker let out a stream of expletives, and his hand chopped at Cory's side until Cory released his neck. Parker threw a punch, but Cory ducked. Cory snagged him around the waist and threw him into the wall, then landed a punch to Parker's jaw. Parker's elbow slammed Cory under the chin. Cory saw stars and heard his brother's voice. He was being pulled, but he couldn't see. And then he heard Logan yell "shit" before the lights went out completely.

When he came to he was in Logan's office, lying on the couch with an icepack on his face. The lights were off and only the glow of the computer lit the room. He saw from the clock he'd been out for three hours.
He sat up, and his head pounded. He stood and staggered to the door. The crowd had thinned. His father and Logan and his *mother* were alone at the bar, so he made his way across the room.

Logan drafted him his favorite brew and placed a pint on the counter. Cory took the seat next to his mother and took a long draw on the beer. He cradled his aching forehead and his jaw in one hand.

Logan pulled out a towel, loaded it with ice, and handed it across the bar.

"Sucker punch. Parker apologized when it was clear that you wouldn't be waking up for a while."

Cory grunted, but he pressed the ice against his face.

"You wanna talk about what's going on with you?" He heard his mother's voice, smooth like silk, as it filtered through the pain in his head.

Cory shot her a hateful look. She couldn't be serious—she wanted to *parent* him now? He was nearly thirty; she'd missed his parenting years. He huffed out a no and went back to nursing his head.

"You ever going to forgive me for what I did?"

He wanted to give her another unequivocal no, but he managed to say, "Don't flatter yourself. This has nothing to do with you."

"Oh, I think it might have a little to do with me."

Logan was watching them. Shit, just what had he told their mother?

Logan had always been too smart. He would pick up on stuff nobody realized they were projecting and have it all sorted out before anyone else could even blink.

His mother swiveled her barstool toward him. "I never apologized to you because I didn't want to experience your rejection. It is, of course, within your rights to refuse my apology."

Christ, he didn't want to hear this now.

"I'm not looking for vindication, I just want you to know that I live with the memory of your tear-stained face and your clinging body every day."

Damn, he really didn't want to hear this. And he didn't want her talking about how he'd clung to her, especially not in front of Logan and his dad. Angry, he swung around. And saw her face.

Tears were coursing down her cheeks. Silent tears one after the other. Suddenly his father put an arm around her and she buried her face to his chest.

He'd never seen his mother cry. Not ever.

"Son, things happened that I regret. I need to apologize to you for not being there for you when I drove your mother away."

His mother placed her hands on his father's cheeks, "Cliff, you're not going to take all the blame, we were both at fault."

Both of his parents now stared into his eyes. It was a strange event and he couldn't remember the last time it happened, if ever.

His mother spoke, "My leaving had nothing to do with you, Cory. Still, I would give everything to go back to that day and do it differently. To make you understand so that there was never a doubt in your mind." Her hand went to his shoulder. "I'd like to be part of your life again, and if you ever want that, I'll be here." She stood and made her way to the restroom.

Well, shit. He didn't know what to do with that. Best to push it back for the present.

He stared Logan down with narrowed eyes. Logan wore a poker face, and his lips were tighter than a lug nut.

"You know where she is."

Logan didn't deny or confirm, just remained stoic.

His father looked at Logan. "Do you know where she is?"

Still his face was stone.

Cory was beyond frustrated and not in the mood to play games. If Logan knew where Brook was, he was going to get that information. "Logan, I need you to tell me."

Logan filled a glass with ice, topped it off with water. And then he drank. Only then did he say, "For the record, she swore me to secrecy. But I think I can see how this needs to play out and, lucky for you, that will require that I tell you."

Cory's lips tightened, and he was about to fly across the bar and slug his brother when Logan threw out his hand.

"You've behaved like an idiot. She didn't want to leave, but she couldn't stay and risk losing you forever. If I'm about to betray her trust, I need to know what's at stake."

"What's at stake is your pretty face. Tell me where she is!"

"See, that's not going to do it for me, brother. I told you that I liked Brook. And I'm committed to her welfare. What I need to know is are *you* committed to her at all costs?"

Cory fisted his hands in his hair. What the hell was wrong with everybody?

"Will you do right by her?"

Fear seared his gut as he met his brother's unrelenting gaze. "I would give my life for that woman. Please," he begged. "Please help me get her back." Unshed tears stung his eyes.

His father put one arm around him. He was falling apart.

Logan said, "She took a job at the greyhound park near Galveston."

"Galveston? Why?"

Logan looked at their father, but Cory just waved him on. "Logan . . ."

"Because she's pregnant with your child and didn't want to tell you for fear that it would force you to do something that would make you unhappy."

"What?" Brook was pregnant? Heat washed over him, then ice pounded into him, the twin assault leaving him sweating and shaking.

His mind flashed to her with her animals and how committed and attuned to their needs she always was. Not just to their needs but his as well. She was loyal, he knew that. Deep in his heart he knew she'd never willingly leave him. She'd handle their child with that same fierce loyalty and dedication. Then his mind flashed an image of her with a large round belly. He yearned to be next to that woman, to hold that woman, to love that woman, and the child growing in her womb, their child.

Had he actually told her he'd never have children, that he didn't want them? The truth of it was he'd give his left nut to watch her grow large and round with his child. He'd have an entire litter with her.

Logan looked to their father and back to Cory, slapped the bar, and said, "So . . . road trip to Texas?"

"Great idea, son. Let's all three go, shall we?"

"All four of us," his mother said from behind him.

Their father turned to place his arm around her. "That's right, after all this is supposed to be a date." He kissed her chastely on the mouth.

He didn't have time to stop and process what was going on with his parents. "I want to leave tonight," Cory said, his voice nearly as shaky as his hand.

Logan replied, "Let me get Cal in here to run the bar."

***

Cal and Chloe both showed up to oversee the bar. They approached Cory, Logan, and their parents, hand in hand.

Cory's dad placed his large hand on Chloe's stomach and asked, "How's my grandbaby doing?"

Chloe said, "He is very naughty, causing his mother to be up all night with indigestion."

Cal smiled. "And momma's indigestion keeps daddy up."

Cory was riveted on the scene playing out in front of him. He so badly wanted what Cal had that his body began to hum like an engine at the thought of having all he never knew he wanted. But he wanted it, all of it, and he wanted it bad.

This was what had been missing his entire life, what he'd feared would always be missing. Unconditional love and devotion. And now it was right in front of him, his if he didn't blow it.

As Chloe was giving out hugs all around, Cal asked, "So what's goin' on?"

Logan said, "Our Cory here has fucked up royally."

Cal's brow rose. Cory said, "Before you say anything, I've got a plan to make it right."

Cal raised his hands in surrender. "Hey, I'm not saying a word. So what's the plan?"

They informed Cal and Chloe of Operation Retrieve Brook and Eagle.

Chloe said, "Be prepared, Cory. You can't force her to come back with you. She might be upset. I don't know, if it were me, if I'd be ready to follow you back to Whisky Cove."

Cory shook his head. "She has to come back."

Chloe squeezed his shoulder. "I'm not saying she won't come back, just be prepared. It may take some time for her to come around."

CHAPTER 9

Once they were on the interstate, Cory asked, "How long does it say it'll take?"

Their father was driving and Logan was navigating from the passenger seat. "The GPS says four and a half hours with traffic."

"It'll be almost one in the morning when we arrive. And you're sure you know exactly where she lives?"

"She's renting a place from a friend of mine I hooked her up with."

Cory's body immediately tensed. "You hooked her up with someone?"

Logan looked over his shoulder. "Will you relax? She's an ex-girlfriend of mine."

Cory nodded, relieved. He thought about what Chloe had said. It was true, Brook probably wouldn't be ready to drop everything yet again and follow him home. Unless he had a grand plan. He had just over four hours to come up with a fail proof reason for her to take him back.

***

Cory heard the voice of his mother come to him in a dream. "We're here."

He opened his eyes—no dream. He sat up and looked out of the side window. "Where?"

Logan pointed to a house across the street. "There."

"It's one thirty in the morning," his dad told him from the front seat. "What's your plan?"

His plan was to storm the house and get Brook. But the holes in that plan hit him like the slap of her hand to his face. "I need a ring!"

The four of them stared at one another so long, Cory was afraid his

60

words had cast some kind of spell. Then Logan started laughing.

"Well, that's step one."

Luckily, Cory's father had connections all along the Gulf Coast and plenty of friends willing to do him favors—even after midnight. He made a few calls and within the hour, they were at a jewelry store looking at rings. Unfortunately, Cory wasn't satisfied with any of them.

"They're beautiful, Mr. Winters, truly, but I can't go to her with any of these." Cory slowly blew out a long breath of air.

His father ran a finger across a few of the rings and asked, "What's the problem?"

"These are too big, too showy, too . . . gaudy. I need something original, something vintage." Cory looked into the eyes of the shop owner. "My Brook has freckles and thick chestnut hair with copper highlights. Her skin is bronze, her eyes are a luminous green—unless she's overcome with desire, and then they darken to a color between gold and bronze. She never wears make-up or perfume," Cory shook his head. "Doesn't have to. She dresses simply and there is nothing fake about her."

All eyes were on Cory. Logan was actually recording him with his phone's camera. Cory blushed and said, "I think with her bronze skin we can rule out anything that isn't yellow gold."

Mr. Winters tapped his chin, his eyes seeing something other than what was laid out on the counter. "I think I have something in the back. It belonged to my grandmother."

When Cory saw the ring, he knew it was the one. It was classically beautiful with an antique emerald, and diamonds in the shape of a flower. The center stone matched the color of Brook's eyes, and the sides were a delicate swirl pattern. Cory smiled brightly, excited and relieved. "This is perfect. Just perfect." He held it out for his mother to see. "Don't you think it's perfect?"

"It's beautiful."

He turned back to Mr. Winters. When he saw the specialty box the man had pulled the ring from, his gut clenched. "You said it belonged to your grandmother. Is it for sale?"

"It isn't."

Cory's breath caught.

"Isn't for sale that is." Mr. Winters placed the ring in a new velvet box. He looked to the St. Martin clan and then grasped Cory's father's hand. "Without your father's assistance, I wouldn't be standing before you today. Your father is a good man. I want you to have the ring."

He nodded. "Good to see you again, Cliff."

Cory's dad nodded back and simply replied, "Knox."

Cory and Logan both looked from one man to the other. They had a connection that ran deep, that much was clear. Cory would ask his father about it another time, but for now he was simply grateful the relationship existed.

He looked to the shop owner who'd given up his night and passed on a family heirloom, all for him. All for love. His eyes swam with tears. "Thank you, sir. You should know, your ring is going to a great lady, one who loves as generously as you do."

***

They killed some time at a twenty-four hour diner, then drove back and waited a little longer in the SUV outside Brook's temporary home. Finally, when Cory couldn't wait any longer, he said, "I'm ready, let's go."

The plan was simple. His dad would carry a bouquet of blue hydrangeas. Cory had seen Brook worry over the hydrangea bushes in front of her home in Whisky Cove and occasionally cut some and bring them inside. Cory's father would offer her the flowers. Logan would film the proposal, and of course Cory would be on bended knee. They all barreled out of the SUV and turned toward the house. His mother stayed seated.

Cory leaned in and said, "Mom?"

"I'll just wait here."

"No, Mom. I need you with me."

Her face went instantly from stormy weather to a warm, lazy summer day, and her smile caressed him, easing some of his worry. "Come on, Mom. We can kiss and *ooh* and *aah* later. Right now I need to see Brook."

It was straight up seven when Cory rang the bell. From his vantage point on bended knee, he first heard the clacking of Eagle's nails on the tile, then the unmistakable sound of the door latch cracking open. In cutoff jeans and a tank top, the love of his life stood staring out at him, wiping the sleep out of her eyes.

Her eyes remained wide as they passed from Cory to his father and mother and then to Logan.

Eagle whimpered, but he didn't leave Brook's side. He too looked from Cory to the others and then back to Cory.

Cory took a deep breath, "Brook, I can't make a move without thinking of you. The thought of never seeing you again makes me crazy with regret. There were things you needed to hear from me, things you deserved to hear. I'm in love and I don't know how to do it. It's painful and it hurts and I'm terrified. I'm out of control, and I hate that. I'm paralyzed without you. The only cure is you so if you run, I will always come after you. I'd walk through a wildfire to get to you."

Brook gasped, one hand at her lips and one at her breast. God, he was botching this, but he was speaking from the heart.

"I see your freckles whenever I close my eyes. In my dreams I feel your hair cascading down my chest, and I seek the heat of your body."

62

Brook blushed, but he needed her to know everything that was in his heart, no holding back. At least her response said that she was feeling something.

"I took you for granted when you lifted me up and taught me how to live, love, and forgive. I see so clearly what I hadn't seen before. You saved me. And I need you to keep me warm. Please, I'd kill to have you back, but I want life, not death. I need you, every inch of you, including our beautiful, wonderful, already much loved child that grows in your belly."

He cracked the velvet box open and removed the ring. He offered it to her. "I don't know how to tell you that if you marry me I'll spend the rest of my days loving every ounce of your beautiful body, mind, and spirit. But I will do it. Maybe not perfectly, but thoroughly." He held both of her hands in his. "Please say yes, Brook."

Eagle woofed and looked from Brook to Cory. Then Eagle stepped forward and licked Cory square on the mouth. Laughter erupted all around. Brook lowered herself to her knees and into Cory's waiting arms. Her hands went into his hair, and they kissed passionately on the stoop with Cory's father, mother, and brother standing right there next to them. When they pulled apart, Cory placed the ring on her finger and a kiss atop both.

His dad offered Brook the flowers and said, "Brook, I like it when St. Martin men marry up. It makes the stock much better." He winked at her. She laughed, and he helped her up. Cory jumped up right beside her.

"Welcome to the family," Logan said. "St. Martins are all a little looney, but you knew that already."

"I did. I guess that means I fit right in."

Cory stepped back when his mother moved in to hug Brook, but he heard her whisper, "I'm so glad he came to his senses."

Cory moved in for his own hug and kissed Brook again, this time a chaste kiss on each cheek. "You're coming home with me." She nodded serenely, just as she had at their first meeting.

Packing up took no time at all, and they were back on the road in less than an hour.

In the back seat of the SUV, Brook sat curled in Cory's lap with her head under his chin. They stayed connected the entire ride back to Whisky Cove. Every half hour or so, Cory would kiss her on the head or cheek and whisper his love in her ear.

Brook stared at her ring often, occasionally holding it up to the light. "It's beautiful. How did you know what to get?"

He smiled down at her in his lap. "I just thought of you."

Logan had his phone out and passed it to her. "Actually, Brook, here is exactly how it went down."

She hit play on the phone. Logan had shot in close-up, so Cory knew she could see the emotion play out across his face and in his eyes. She watched the video five times. Huge teardrops splashed from her eyes and onto the screen.

Cory whispered, "We better give it back, huh? You're gonna drown Logan's phone. That's not a very nice thing to do." Brook laughed through her tears.

It took over five hours to get back, so when they got to the estate, they took Eagle and Teddy, who had been only too happy to greet them, to stretch their legs.

They were out by the pecan grove when Cory said, "Eagle is no longer available to be an adopted companion."

"Oh yeah, why is that?"

"Because he belongs here with our family."

Brook began to cry. Cory lifted her chin. "Hey, what's this." He kissed away her tears.

"Nothing bad, I was just thinking about the last time I belonged to a family. It was before my parents died. That was the last time I truly belonged."

"You'll never have to worry about that again, baby." He laughed and picked her up, turning them in circles until she squealed. "In fact, you'll probably get sick of all the family you're about to acquire." She laughed again, and Cory sucked her bottom lip into his mouth. "I need to be inside you. Connected."

With the dogs secure in the fence, Brook looked up at Cory and said, "Deer stand."

"You read my mind."

They climbed into the stand and each removed their clothing, until only love was left between them.

***

That night, Cory was seated at the kitchen table at his house. His dad was out and it was just them, *his* family. Eagle and Teddy lay at his feet, and Brook was busy making dinner. Cory offered up a prayer of thanks. He'd almost lost Brook; that thought had his throat closing up and squeezing off his air. He gasped and shook his head to rid himself of the worry. Brook was by his side in an instant, a bowl of crawfish etouffee in her hands.

"Hey, I'm here." She set the bowl on the table and took his cheeks in her palms, lifting his face. She placed a tender kiss on his lips. "We'll live our lives together, you and me. Forever."

The words she spoke healed and cleansed Cory. She straddled his lap, and he inhaled her essence long and deep. His hand slipped under her tank top, and he spread his palm across her abdomen. "I want children. Lots of children. I want them all to look like you."

Brook frowned. "But I want them to look like you."

Cory grinned. "We'll see what we can do. And by the way, I love you." Eagle came up to stand by the chair in his guardian's pose. Cory turned to him. "Will you relax? I'm about to show your mother how much I love her."

Eagle stood and placed his snout between them. "You're going to have to explain to Eagle how things work around here," he told Brook.

She smiled as she rubbed her face into his neck. His hands were caressing her bare back, under her shirt. She started purring.

"Hey, you're going to be Brook St. Martin. Do you like the way that sounds?"

She lifted her head, pouting, "I thought you would become Corrigan Walker."

Cory's brow furrowed as he stared into Brook's emerald-green gaze. "Is that what you want?"

"More than you know." She winked at him and placed her arms around his neck and sucked his earlobe into her mouth.

"What the hell, I'll be Cory Walker. It has a nice ring."

Brook smiled against his skin. "What happened to my challenging man?"

He kissed her softly. "Baby, if you think I'm not going to insist you take my name, you've gone delusional." Brook giggled.

She smiled against his mouth. "I'm going to become a St. Martin. I can't think of anything I want more." His erection pressed into her crotch. "Well, there may be one thing I want more than your name."

***

Brook was so happy that she *could* be delusional. Only she wasn't.

She'd been given everything she ever wanted. The child growing in her belly would be a part of her and she a part of it. It would be a blood connection, and she'd cherish her child until her dying breath. It wasn't lost on her that in time roots would grow under and around her until she was also entwined with the St. Martin family. She'd suddenly gone from being an orphan with no family to a woman with so much family her heart swelled from the abundance of love she'd received from them already.

With Cory's admission of love and his commitment to spend the rest of his life devoted to her, she felt absolute peace. If she fell, if she faltered, he would catch her. Before she'd been alone, but now there was Cory. And family. And children. Generations to look forward to, dreams to plan for. She quivered at the future of possibilities.

On the drive home, when Cory'd cradled her in his lap, he'd whispered that she was the closest to heaven he'd ever be and that for her he wanted to be the strongest version of himself. He'd said she'd taught him how to live, love, and forgive, but he'd made her feel wanted and needed, given her life a purpose. She'd needed a purpose for so long.

She tipped her head down when he pressed his palm against her belly.

"There's a baby in here, Brook. A baby we made."

The awe in his voice had tears gathering in her eyes. She cupped her hand over his.

This man had given her everything. That she got to spend the rest of her life loving him and raising his children was a bonus.

She'd come back to Whiskey Cove because it was the place where her happiest memories rested. It seemed that tradition would continue. Her life had been a journey that led her back to the beginning. She loved beginnings and, in time, she knew she would come to love middles and endings too. She couldn't wait to live the rest of her life as Brook St. Martin.

EXCERPT *SHATTER*

Logan pulled into the gravel lot of La Bella Luna and jumped out of his truck. It was between lunch and dinner, so not much was shaking inside the restaurant. He walked toward the bar, where a young woman, her back to him, was filling salt and pepper shakers.

"Excuse me. I'm looking for Jessica Hunter."

"You're late," the woman responded with a terse voice.

Logan leaned in closer. "How's that?"

Louder she repeated, "I said you're late."

She had spunk. Or maybe she was majorly crabby. He hoped it was spunk. He didn't want to partner with some bitchy woman. Whistling and studying the near empty restaurant, he said, "Shall I come back at a less busy time?"

He saw her neck tighten. Or maybe it was her back straightening into a board as she forced herself to curb her response. Whatever it was, he noticed the movement. And he noticed because he was focusing on the rust-colored hair that was tied into a thick knot at the nape of her neck. Pretty hair. Too pretty to be knotted tight—

She turned, and his breathing hitched. She was incredible. Truly breathtaking. And he immediately knew he was in trouble. Logan was a sucker for redheads, and with her milky skin and sizzling blue eyes melting into him, his heart started racing. Her lips were parted. Her top teeth peeked out and landed on her thick bottom lip as she began to nervously chew at it.

His mouth instantly wanted to do the same, to nibble and taste and explore her lips and the heat of her mouth.

She took him in with equal curiosity, scanning him from head to toe as her long dark lashes created shadows across her pink cheeks. He wanted to run his fingers through the lustrous hair so thick she had to double clip it.

There was an abundance of it, and he thought he caught a scent of apple cinnamon. She was wearing black shorts and a white T-shirt with a nametag that read *Jessie*. She untied the black apron from her waist and motioned for him to follow her. He had no problem following those twitching hips.

Her office was full of file cabinets and everything needed to run her business. In the corner were stacks of T-shirts, shorts, and aprons. Logan assumed it was the standard uniform. A box of invoices and a ten-key adding machine sat on her desk next to an accounting log. The space was considerably messy, given how clean and organized the restaurant was. He took the chair next to her desk while she let out a grunt and dropped into her desk chair. A bare light bulb screwed into the ceiling was the only light in the office.

Jessie cleared her throat. "Under the circumstances, I don't think this partnership is a good idea after all."

Logan leaned back into his chair and crossed his arms over his chest. "Is that so?"

She raised a dark copper brow. "Yes, I do believe it is."

She was certainly cute the way she asserted herself, restrained and calm. He wondered if she held herself back like that in the sack. He smirked and allowed a laugh to break free.

***

Jessica thought Logan St. Martin couldn't possibly think she would enter into a business partnership with him. The man looked like a bum. A cute bum, but a bum nonetheless.

He wore cargo shorts and a green T-shirt bearing an image of a frothy mug of beer. The T-shirt's caption read *The Drinking Games, only one will be left standing*. His leather sandals had flopped—no flipping, just *flop, flop, flop*—all the way down the hallway to her office. To top it off, he was late and sarcastic. She knew his type. Nothing was as important to him as his fun and games. He'd be out of business within the year. Well, he could forget joining up with her—there was no way she'd have him add dead weight to her existing financial problems. She worked her ass off to make this place work and still her efforts might not be enough.

Women probably threw themselves at him because of his long sandy blond hair worn in fashionable disarray and his immense green eyes. He was tall and slim, with all-over facial hair clipped close to his square face. Damn, why'd he have to look the way he looked? Whiskers were Jessie's weakness.

So yeah, damn him and his sexy smirk.

"This may be a joke to you, Mr. St. Martin, but this is my life. I won't have you traipsing in here whenever the spirit moves you. If I can't rely on you to be on time or to at least give me a courtesy call, then I won't be able to trust you in a partnership."

She stood to leave, but he caught her by the wrist.

"Sit down." His voice was authoritative, and his smirk had been replaced with a piercing stare.

"Excuse me?"

"I know you need this opportunity to make your business thrive. You won't find another distributor willing to provide the product up front for no cost until you deliver the goods. I understand sweat equity, but I assume you're out on the floor filling salt and pepper shakers and napkin dispensers because money is tight. I take it you wait tables all night as well, that's why you're behind on paperwork in here. Look, I know business. It's only my first year, but I'm operating considerably in the black. You need my help. And call me Logan. I'll be calling you Jessie."

She straightened her posture and tilted her head high at his words, but she was smart enough to keep her mouth shut. After all, what he'd said was true. She did need his stupid beer.

"Are you prepared to hear my proposal?"

"I'll hear it." She'd extend him that courtesy, at least. She sat back at her desk.

"I'm looking to expand my distribution into certain socioeconomic markets. Your restaurant fits my criteria. I plan to use this place as a beta site for the restaurant marketability of my products."

"A beta what?"

"Beta site. I haven't distributed in restaurants before; yours will be the first. I'll use La Bella Luna as a test site to iron out any kinks that may arise."

"So essentially I'm your guinea pig."

Logan smiled. "Exactly. But what you'll get out of the collaboration is worth it. As I said before, I'll not charge you up front and only cost after. It's a win-win for you, but I might suggest changing your marketing and distribution avenues."

"Oh, I don't think I have much of those things. We exist on word of mouth and if people want to eat, they just walk through the door."

"That may have worked before but in this climate, you need what works today. And that means changes. For example, how much profit do you make from home delivery?"

"We don't deliver."

"How many calls would you say you get per day for delivery inquiries?"

"I wouldn't know."

"Hmm, you might want to keep track and consider offering a delivery service. It would be another market to expand into with next to no startup costs. And the market has started to turn, with people spending more on takeout food. You need to capitalize on that upshift. A radio blurb doesn't cost that much, and it would do wonders to alert the public that there is an Italian restaurant tucked down this dead-end road. Tracking how customers hear about the restaurant is also a good idea."

Jessie exhaled a deep breath. She clumsily plopped her head on her forearm and rested it on the desk in utter defeat. She sniffled.

Logan was on his feet immediately, "Are you okay?"

Her head rose, her eyes flooded with tears. "No, I'm not okay." She sobbed. "You come in here with your aggressive eagerness and start throwing your big words around and picking apart everything I'm doing." She was crying harder now, huge tears streaming down her face and falling to her lap. "And the thing of it is, you're exactly right. I'm completely out of my element here. Since Brandon died, everything's been steadily deteriorating, and I've been powerless to stop the slide." She sagged in her chair on a sniff.

Logan squatted between her legs and looked up at her. She supposed he was trying to be comforting and non-threatening, but he was in her space. She eased back a bit.

"Who's Brandon?" he asked.

"Brandon was my husband. He died five years ago. We'd had the restaurant for a while, and it was thriving. Then things started to change."

Logan used his index finger to lift her face so they were eye to eye. "How about I help you and you help me? I'll track a few things, see if there might be some sensible changes you can make to yield a higher profit. In turn, you'll let me sell my brew. What do you say?"

Jessie nodded. They were so close she could feel his heat and smell his scent. He smelled of the outdoors, of grass, gasoline, and leather. And hops. She imagined she smelled the scent of honeyed hops on his skin.

His eyes were like jewels, their color a pure, clear green, and his sincere demeanor was reassuring. He was very masculine, and her stomach fluttered as she imagined how his body would feel above hers. Her attraction to him was immediate, and she wondered what it would be like to kiss him. She didn't have to wonder long—he leaned in and placed his lips on hers, slowly sucking her bottom lip into his mouth. His tongue slid past her lips and teeth as he tasted her mouth. Her tongue tentatively twined with his. He tasted of yeast, and she idly wondered how much beer he drank on any given day. With a smooth move, he sucked on her tongue. Without warning, she became wet with desire.

It had been too long—way too long—since she'd felt passion. Of their own will, her hands slid under his shirt until she was touching his warm skin. He was smooth and slim, and with her fingertips she traced the long lean section of his torso. Needing to see him, she pulled his shirt over his head. His shorts hung low on his hips, so low she could see his pelvic muscles and the light trail of hair that led into his shorts. Had she thought him cute? A colossal understatement. He was bronzed male perfection. She was entranced, and in response, her body beckoned for his touch.

ABOUT THE AUTHOR

Gina Watson is author of the St. Martin Family Saga. She lives in Texas where she leads a double life: university instructor by day, romance writer by night. She loves to be contacted by readers to discuss all things romance.

Connect with Gina Watson online:
https://twitter.com/ginawatsongina
https://www.facebook.com/ginawatsonauthor
https://www.goodreads.com/user/show/6713553-gina
http://ginawatson.net/

Reviews: Please help spread the word. Review the book at Amazon, twitter, facebook, goodreads, or via email. Tag Gina so she can read your reviews and give her thanks.

Keep in touch: Join Gina Watson's email list at ginawatson@mac.com to receive alerts regarding sweepstakes, contests, giveaways, and upcoming book releases.

GINA WATSON'S BOOKS

ST. MARTIN FAMILY SAGA
SCORE
SHAMELESS
SHATTER
SUITED
SMOLDER

THE SAGA CONTINUES IN
THE EMERGENCY RESPONDERS TRILOGY:
SIZZLE
SECURE
SOOTHE

COMING 2014

25590718R30048

Made in the USA
Charleston, SC
08 January 2014